I0747358

ALEX CAGE
CLEAN FAST-PACED ACTION THRILLERS

JOIN THE READER'S LIST

Get the latest releases and exclusive giveaways - sign up to the Alex Cage Reader List:

www.AlexCage.com/signup

ALSO BY ALEX CAGE

Orlando Black Series

Carolina Dance

Bayside Boom

Bet on Black

Leroy Silver Series

Contracts & Bullets

Aloha & Bullets

Politics Thieves & Bullets

Get the latest releases and exclusive giveaways, sign up to the Alex Cage Reader List.

www.AlexCage.com/signup

RANCID BADGES

ALEX CAGE

RANCID BADGES

ONE

Behind bars wasn't where a good cop should be. But it's where Derrick Nash found himself. It made no sense. He was completely innocent, yet there he stood in a six-by-eight cell like a common criminal. Nash played the scenario repeatedly in his head, hoping to identify what went wrong. He had nothing. Dressed in full police uniform, Nash rubbed his hands across his brush cut faded hair, then sat on the single bunk and faced the wall with his forehead in his palms. Anxiety filled his body, but he was thankful to be separated from the characters in the general holding cell. A perk of being a cop, which Nash didn't take for granted.

A paunchy officer sporting a full beard and a low-fade approached Nash's cell. With his chubby, mocha-toned hand, he reached through the cell's door and grabbed a bar.

"Yo, Derrick," the officer said.

Nash's eyebrows furrowed as he stood. "Chris?" He walked toward the cell door. "What's going on?"

"Someone wanna talk to you."

Nash winced.

Chris leaned close to the bars. "It's Lieutenant Barnhill," he whispered, before pointing at the back side of his hand, which was a shade darker than Nash's. "Like most of us, the lieutenant thinks there's something shady about your situation." He removed a key and inserted it into the door lock.

"Barnhill's here this time of night?"

Chris nodded.

"Good. I've been racking my brain trying to—"

Chris put a finger to his own mouth. "Keep it down," he said while opening the door. "The walls may have ears."

Nash nodded.

Chris led him through the cellblock to a set of double doors. The chubby officer waved a card in front of a panel near the door, then pressed numbers on the keypad next to it. A buzz flowed from the door as it clicked open. The two men entered a dark hall on their way to another door at the far end. They stepped into a corridor. Fluorescent lights hummed above as Nash took the lead and followed the corridor to an office. The office door was ajar. Nash nudged it open fully, then walked inside with Chris behind him.

A man with a salt-and-pepper mini-afro and a goatee of the same flavor sat behind a bulky desk. Nash knew the man as Lieutenant Stan Barnhill, his commanding officer and friend. A direct and fair man, who understood politics and knew how to deal with bureaucracy—which were essential skills in their line of work. A reality Nash was quickly coming to terms with.

"Thank you, Chris," Barnhill said in a no-nonsense tone. "I'll take it from here."

"Okay," Chris said. "Be around if you need me."

Chris left the office, and as the door shut behind him, Barnhill stood from his chair.

"Derrick. I need to know what's going on," he said.

Nash shrugged his shoulders. "You probably know just as much as I do. What did Moore tell you?"

Moore was the officer who had arrested Nash six hours earlier. Nash had received a tip from an informant right before his shift ended. But when he arrived at the address the informant gave him, Nash found a completely different situation from what he expected.

"He said he caught you inside a vacant house with the drugs and money that went missing from evidence three days ago," Barnhill answered.

Nash sighed, then shook his head. "I had nothing to do with that. I was following a lead in the Jackson case."

"The Frank Jackson case? That's a murder case—you're not a detective yet—you're still a beat cop. What are you doing working the Jackson case?"

Nash cocked his head to the side and bounced a shoulder. He opened his mouth but couldn't find the words.

"It doesn't matter," Barnhill continued. "Moore's working that case, but you knew that already."

Nash glanced at Barnhill, then at the floor. Barnhill exhaled, circled his desk, and stood next to Nash.

"Look me in the eye," Barnhill said.

Nash turned to him and complied.

"Did you take the drugs and money from evidence?"

"I already told you, no," Nash said.

They continued to stare at one another. Both looked away a moment shy of it becoming too awkward.

Barnhill nodded. "I believe you."

"Good, because I'm telling the truth," Nash said.

"I know."

Nash's eyebrows furrowed. "What? How?"

Ignoring the question, Barnhill grabbed a set of keys, cell phone, and wallet from his desk and handed them to Nash before turning for the office door. "Let's get you home," he said. "I've already handled the necessary paperwork, but the department's gonna keep your badge and gun until we get more answers about—" Barnhill shook his head. "About this misunderstanding," he continued. "I know you. You're a good cop, and I'm not gonna have you sitting in a cell all night. Especially while in uniform."

Without question, Nash placed his items in their respective pockets. Since he had a get-out-of-jail-free card, he figured it'd be wise to take it. He followed Barnhill through the door and across a dim office floor scattered with empty desks. They reached the receptionist area where Barnhill said goodnight to a completely bald, bearded officer sitting behind a bulletproof glass partition.

"I'm in the back," Barnhill told Nash as the back door buzzed. Barnhill waved at the officer behind the partition as he exited. Nash glanced back at the officer and noticed the bearded man staring at him.

"Never seen him. Is he new?" Nash asked Barnhill once they were outside.

"Yeah. He's only been on for two weeks, working the front and sometimes in evidence. You know the Atlanta PD has a lot of turnover, especially at this precinct."

Nash followed Barnhill through the parking lot under the dull glow of an overhead lamppost. Two other lampposts were staggered throughout the parking lot. The lights did a good job of illuminating one or two cars from the handful of parked vehicles, but left many areas in the shadows. The parking lot was publicly accessible but fenced in. Two open gates on the north side allowed access in and out. Further west, beyond the fence line, sat a small, vacant lot. To the east stood a fifteen-foot wall. Tall, lit buildings in the distance encompassed the station. A city seemingly at rest, but not asleep.

When the men reached a silver pickup truck, Barnhill pointed his thumb at the passenger side. "Get in," he told Nash.

Nash circled the hood while Barnhill opened the driver's side door. As Nash reached for his own door handle, a loud boom stuffed the air and rattled his upper body.

Barnhill grunted, then palmed his side and fell sprawled across the driver's seat and center console. Two more blasts roared, followed by a heavy thump and the back driver's side window shattering. Nash ducked inside the truck and pulled Barnhill out through the passenger side. The lieutenant groaned as Nash laid him on the cold pavement.

Nash felt warm liquid dripping down his hand. It was blood.

"You're hit," he said while grabbing Barnhill's hand and pressing it against the lieutenant's wound located just below his ribcage. "Keep pressure here."

Nash peeked through the busted window and saw two male silhouettes emerging from the shadows near a parked SUV. The figures slowly approached the truck's driver's side. Another blast erupted, and a bullet crashed into the truck's door jamb, just inches from Nash's head.

Nash ducked. "There's two of 'em," he told Barnhill.

"Take my gun," Barnhill said, grunting as he reached for the firearm on his hip.

"Hey, I'll get it," Nash said while unholstering Barnhill's pistol. "Don't move."

Rising to a crouch, Nash aimed the pistol through the broken window and fired three rounds. One man clutched his shoulder and knelt while his partner stooped and scurried to his aid. The glimmer from an overhead lamppost caught the man as he swooped in to help. He wore dark jeans, a dark shirt, and had a piece of material covering his lower face. The darkness made it nearly impossible to see any details beyond that.

Nash sank back behind the car. "I think I got one."

When Barnhill didn't answer, Nash looked over and saw the lieutenant huffing labored breaths. Barnhill coughed, and his lips moved. Nash arched down and turned his ear to the lieutenant.

"Don—don't trust anyone," Barnhill muttered.

Commotion flowed from the station. Nash looked through the window and saw multiple figures racing from the station's back door. He glanced at where he last saw his attackers, but they were no longer there.

Barnhill moaned. "Go," he said before fainting.

Nash checked his lieutenant's neck and found a pulse. Peeking through the window, he saw Chris along with the reception officer and one other uniform approaching the truck. Nash stayed low, hurried outside the gate nearest to him and to a corner in the shadows. He watched as Chris circled the truck, knelt, and examined Barnhill.

"Call dispatch!" he yelled to the other two officers. "Tell them to send a paramedic now!"

Nash shook his head at the sight. A lump formed in his throat, and his breathing became shallow. He wanted to go back, but he knew his lieutenant told him not to trust anyone for a reason. Nash captured another glance of Barnhill lying on the pavement with Chris craned over him. Nash closed his eyes and looked away. The impulse to take one final look tempted him, but he stuffed his pistol in his front waistband and hustled toward the main street instead.

TWO

After a three-block hike, followed by a fourteen-minute Lift ride, then another two-block hike, Nash arrived at the front door of his townhouse. He lived in a small suburb located five minutes outside of Midtown Atlanta. The glow from his front door lamp aided him as he fished out his jangling keyring and found the door's keyhole. Looking to his right, then left, Nash scanned the area before unlocking the door and entering.

Once inside, he flicked on the light switch. The lamp in the corner to his right brightened the room. Nash quickly locked the door behind himself and headed straight to the bathroom sink, where he scrubbed Barnhill's blood from his hands. He splashed water on his face, then stripped out of his uniform and wiped his body with a washcloth. Nash stared at himself in the mirror, regretting ever getting involved with the Jackson murder case. Knowing he didn't have much time before his colleagues came knocking on his door, he stopped his pondering and went to his bedroom. After shrugging into a pair of jeans, a T-shirt, jacket, and boots, he removed his spare pistol, a Glock 17, and magazines from a lockbox under his bed. Before sliding the box back under, he placed Barnhill's gun inside. Standing, Nash stuffed his Glock 17 into his front waistband. The spare magazines, he settled inside his pocket.

Four knocks on the front door welcomed Nash as he stepped into his living area. His heart skipped a beat. He removed his gun and slowly approached the door. His breathing grew heavier with each step. He relaxed when he recognized the person through the door's peephole. He unlocked the door and opened it. A fit woman standing shoulder-height to him brushed past on her way inside.

Her natural, twisted bobbed hair bounced as she turned to Nash. "You're not answering your mobile," she said with a slight British accent.

Nash poked his head outside and looked around before ducking back inside and shutting the door.

"Yeah, I know," he said while locking the door.

The woman stared at Nash with her shoulders hunched and palms facing the ceiling. Her dark almond skin radiated under the corner lamp's glow. "So, what happened?"

"What are you doing here?"

"What do you mean? You said you were following up on something and would call me back in an hour, but never did."

"I was arrested."

"Why? What for?"

Nash shook his head. "Not sure."

The woman's eyebrows furrowed. "What?"

"You can't be here right now."

"Why not?"

"We'll talk about it later," Nash said as he stepped to the door.

"I'm not leaving until you tell me what happened."

Nash had only known the woman for a week, but in all of their conversations he picked up on an air of stubbornness. Knowing that about her, and the fact he didn't have much time, Nash decided it would be best to compromise a little.

"Okay. I'll explain everything, but let's go." Nash opened the door and scanned the area before walking out.

She followed behind him. "Where are we going?"

Nash locked the door. "I'll tell you on the way," he said. "My car's in the garage. Let's take yours. I'll drive."

"We'll take my car, but I'm driving."

Nash sighed and shook his head before following the woman down the driveway and to her silver Acura TLX parked at the curb. She slid in behind the wheel, and Nash glanced the area over one last time before entering on the passenger side.

The woman brought the engine to life. "So where to?"

"Just outta the neighborhood," Nash instructed. "Once we get to Monroe Road, I'll direct."

She fixed on his face for a moment before dragging the car into gear and pulling off. They drove in silence for a couple of minutes before speaking.

"So, are you going to tell me why you were arrested?" the woman asked.

Nash stared straight ahead. "Like I said, I'm not sure."

"Well, what happened?"

Nash adjusted in the chair. "I received a tip from an informant. When I arrived at the address..."

In that moment, Nash knew what his next move was. He would pay Tony a visit. Nash had been using Tony as an informant for over a year. They met totally by coincidence. Nash was dispatched to a neighborhood in East Atlanta for a mugging. No one wanted to talk. Randomly, Nash pulled Tony out of a crowd across the street from where the mugging took place and offered him cash for information. The information led to an arrest. Nash never thought much of the snitch, but the twerp had a pulse on what was happening on the streets of Atlanta. Mainly because his family ran drugs for some low-level cartels back in the day.

In some ways, Nash felt he had hit a gold mine with Tony.

That was until the fink's information got him set up and arrested. Nash was itching to have a word with him. But he didn't feel it would be a good idea for his female companion to tag along. He didn't care how headstrong she was. It could be dangerous.

"When you arrived at the address, what?" Kristi asked.

Nash said nothing.

She hit the brakes, and Nash jerked forward.

"Hey! Whatchu doing? You crazy?"

She raised an eyebrow. "No—maybe. There's a stop sign, so I stopped."

Nash looked through the windshield and saw the Acura's headlights illuminating the red octagon.

"You never know when a cop is around."

Nash contorted his lips, a gesture that suggested he wasn't entertained by her sarcasm.

"So?" she asked.

Nash sighed. "There was drugs and money inside the house. The same drugs and money that went missing from the department's evidence locker three days ago. Conveniently, there was also a police officer there to arrest me."

The woman dragged a twist of hair behind her ear while glancing at the floorboard.

"You know you can be pushy," Nash told her.

She shrugged. "You told me to drive to Monroe Road. I was waiting for your direction."

"Right."

"Seriously."

"No, I mean, make a right." Nash smiled.

She contorted her lips this time. "The whole situation sounds very shady," she said while making the turn. "Almost like you were set up."

Nash grabbed his chin.

They drove behind a large pickup truck for a mile before hearing sirens. A minute later, red and blue lights streaked across the Acura's hood. Nash slid down in his seat as two squad cars zoomed past in the opposite direction. The Acura continued for another mile. Every few seconds, Nash either glanced at the back window or checked his side mirror. The woman noticed. They drove for another half a mile before Nash instructed her to make a left turn.

"This seems serious," the woman started. "Maybe we—"

"No, no, no," Nash interrupted. "No we. Once we get to your house, I'm gonna need to borrow a car, and you need to get outta town."

She hit the brakes again, but this time there was no stop sign.

"You are crazy!" Nash said, sitting straight in his seat.

"I'm not leaving town."

"It's dangerous."

"You don't think I know that? I've been telling you that from day one."

"Yeah, but this is—"

"Different? Why? Because you're not sure if you can trust the cops now? I saw the way you ducked when those police cruisers passed."

"You don't understand."

"I understand perfectly. You may be a good cop, but there are also bad ones with rancid badges. If you don't believe me, I can take you back to your place."

Nash looked at her but said nothing.

"Like I told you before, my husband was murdered by cops."

THREE

Nash thought back to when he had first met her. His shift had just ended, and he was leaving the station when he noticed two officers in the bullpen struggling with a handcuffed perp.

"Everything okay?" Nash asked as he approached the situation.

"Yeah, yeah, we can handle this scumbag," a bald officer said.

The other officer, who was taller, shook his head, then walked away toward the break room.

The handcuffed, scruffy, bearded man resisted as the bald officer forced him into a chair. "I'm the scumbag?" the man said. "You harassed me."

"Shut up!" the officer demanded.

"You're nothing but a crooked, donut-eating pig!"

The officer grabbed a fistful of the man's shirt. "Whatchu say?"

Nash placed his hand on the officer's shoulder. "Hey. Calm down, gentlemen."

"This dirtbag better watch his mouth," the officer fumed.

"I'm not the bad guy, you are," the scruffy man asserted.

The officer raised a fist at the man.

Nash grabbed his arm. "Whoa, whoa, whoa," he said while stepping between the officer and the man. He leaned toward the officer's ear. "Not a good look. Go grab a cup of coffee while I talk to him."

The officer fixed on Nash's face before peering over his shoulder at the handcuffed man.

"C'mon, go take a break," Nash encouraged the officer.

The officer nodded and took two steps back. He pointed at the handcuffed man. "You lucky," he said before pivoting away and heading for the break room.

When the officer disappeared into the break room, Nash slid a chair in front of the perp and sat in it.

"What's going on?" he asked.

The scruffy man rolled his eyes.

"Look, I'm trying to help you."

"Yeah right. A cop trying to help me."

"So you're not gonna tell me what's going on?"

"Your co-worker's a jerk. That's what's going on." The man scoffed. "He wouldn't listen to anything I was telling him."

Nash saw the taller officer come from the break room. "What about his partner?" Nash said, nodding in the officer's direction.

The scruffy man glanced at the officer before turning back to Nash and shrugging. "He's more polite, but don't know why he didn't tell his annoying baldheaded partner to calm down."

"Are you more comfortable with him?"

"Yeah, I guess. Just keep that other guy away from me."

Nash stood and waved the officer over. He talked with the tall man and convinced him to process the perp without his partner.

As the officer took the perp to the back for processing, the woman caught Nash's eye. She wore jeans and a long-sleeved button-down shirt. She looked tired, but Nash thought she was stunning. They locked eyes for a moment, then Nash looked away and headed for the back door. He exited and walked across the parking lot. When he was halfway to his car, someone called to him.

"Excuse me, Officer! Wait a minute!" The voice carried a soft, assertive tone, wrapped in a British accent.

Nash turned and saw the woman standing behind him. "Yeah, how can I help you, ma'am?"

"I saw what you did in there," she said.

Nash's eyebrows furrowed.

"For that man. You stood up for him."

Nash shrugged. "Just trying to maintain the peace. You know, do what's right."

The woman took a few steps toward Nash. "You seem to be one of the good ones," she said. "I need your help."

"Okay, well, you can file a report with the station."

The woman quickly shook her head. "No, it has to be you. No one else can know about it."

"I'm sorry, Mrs…"

"Jackson, Kristi Jackson."

Before Nash knew it, he was investigating Frank Jackson's murder. He met and called Kristi almost every day for a week. And now he sat as a passenger in her car, looking into her beautiful, vulnerable, yet strong brown eyes.

"I know what you told me," Nash said. "Which is all the more reason for you to leave."

Kristi glanced at the windshield, closed her eyes, then exhaled before placing her attention back on Nash. "Well, that's not happening, so we have to come up with something else. Or, like I said, I can just take you back to your place."

With his index finger and thumb, Nash pinched his nasal bridge and looked at the floorboard. He sighed. "Okay, you can stay. But you hafta do exactly as I say."

Kristi squinted and nodded. "Yeah, yeah, sure."

"I mean it, Kristi. This is serious. I was already shot at tonight."

She winced. "What—When?"

"I'll tell you all about it when we're outta town?"

She glared at him.

"I'm tired," Nash said with his palms raised in a surrender posture. "I've been up all night, and I think it's best we find a hotel outside of Atlanta."

Kristi nodded, then faced the windshield and gave the Acura some gas. The car accelerated and sped down the dark road. Nash had many thoughts going through his head. Paying his informant a visit was chief among them, but it would have to wait.

FOUR

Hours later, Nash woke in a twin-sized bed. He rubbed his eyes and turned to his side as the late morning sun beamed on his face. Five feet away from him sat a separate twin-size bed. It was unmade. In that moment, Nash recalled that he and Kristi found a motel just outside of Athens. They sat across from each other on the beds, talking. Now, running water flowed from the bathroom. Nash leaned forward, then spun so his feet hung from the side of the bed in the bathroom's direction.

A few seconds later, Kristi stepped from the bathroom, patting her face with a towel. "Oh, you're awake," she said.

"Of course I am."

Kristi smiled. "You fell asleep while we were talking," she said on the way to her bed. "I guess you were exhausted."

Nash yawned. "I wasn't out too long, was I? It's only..." He looked at the clock. "Almost eleven!"

Nash sprang to his feet as Kristi sat across from him.

"Chill," she told him. "Checkout isn't until one."

"I hafta meet someone."

"Who? Is this about the case?"

Nash shrugged. "It's about me being set up. But the two seem connected."

Kristi stood. "I'll go with you."

Nash had his reservations about her tagging along, but he didn't have time to go back and forth with her.

"Okay," he said. "But I'm driving."

Kristi shrugged a shoulder. "Deal."

"Alright then," Nash said on his way to the bathroom.

Twelve minutes later, they were on the road heading toward Atlanta. They stopped at a drive-thru for breakfast, then continued on the road for an hour before arriving at a dilapidated, eight-story apartment building just outside Druid Hills. A few homeless individuals had pitched tents outside the building, and Nash knew many squatted inside. He parked the car at the curb, fifteen yards away from the structure. Kristi's mouth gaped as she surveyed the area. She fixed on a large church a block up across the street.

"Why are we here?" she asked.

"I told you, I hafta meet someone," Nash said.

"Here?" Her nose crinkled.

"Yeah. What? You're scared?"

Kristi winced and kissed her teeth. "No. I grew up near Lambeth, one of the most dangerous boroughs in London. I'm not afraid."

Nash contorted his lips and threw his head back in a half-nod.

"What's that look?"

"Nothing. Just—hard to imagine."

A smirk arched on Kristi's face. "Well, believe it." She cocked her head to the side and stared at Nash through squinted eyes. "Where did you grow up?"

"Not too far from here, believe it or not."

"Oh. So you have family nearby?"

"No, not anymore. I mean, nearby. My mom and dad

retired and moved to North Carolina. My brother's in Florida."

"A brother, huh?"

"Yeah, he's a police officer in Florida."

"Let me guess. Your father was a police officer?"

"Yep."

Kristi nodded. "I'm an only child."

"I know."

"How?"

Nash again contorted his lips and half-nodded.

"There's that look again. What?"

Nash chuckled and shook his head before turning his attention to the windshield. A group walked from the church to a small park across the street. Nash narrowed his sights on a lanky man leaning against a tree near the edge of the park.

"Any chance you'll stay in the car while I go to my meet?" he asked Kristi.

"No. Not a chance."

"Thought so."

They left the car and made their way to the park. A busted chain-link gate greeted them as they passed through and headed toward the back of the grounds. A few disheveled and unpleasant-smelling individuals formed a line near the man at the tree. He had a buzz cut and fair skin. The man smiled, exposing a mouth full of gold teeth as the unkempt individuals stepped to him one at a time, each handing him a small wad of cash. With his head on a swivel, he took the cash and passed them a tiny sac filled with miniature blue rocks.

Nash witnessed this transaction twice before stepping in front of the third person in line.

The man stood from the tree. "Hey. No cut—" He fixed on Nash's face.

"What's up, Tony?" Nash said.

Tony pursed his lips and looked at the ground.

Nash grinned. "We need to—"

Before he could complete his sentence, Tony raced toward the opposite end of the park

"Tony, Tony, don't make it worse," Nash said, dashing after him.

"Hey, wait," Kristi called.

Nash chased Tony through the back gate and out of the park. Kristi trailed behind.

"Why you running, Tony?" Nash yelled as Tony rushed toward the street.

A car horn blared, and the vehicle swerved, barely missing Tony as he crossed. Nash circled the car's hood and chased him toward a corner store. Tony zipped inside the store. Nash followed, dancing around two elderly women as they exited. The scent of hot dogs and the yelps from the store's patrons filled the air as Nash made a right at the chip aisle and pursued Tony to the back exit. The lanky man fought to open the back door. His struggle gave Nash enough time to close the distance between them. As Nash reached for his target, Tony shouldered the door and stumbled outside into an alley. While Tony staggered to his feet, Nash grabbed him and pushed him against the wall, then spun him so they faced each other.

"Why'd you run, Tony?" Nash asked.

"You were chasing me, man," Tony answered between heavy breaths.

Kristi ran into the alley. "Derrick, what's this?" she said, trying to catch her breath. "What's going on?"

"I chased you after you ran," Nash told Tony. "So why'd you run?"

Tony looked away but said nothing.

"Does it have anything to do with the fact you lied to me?"

Tony's eyebrows furrowed. "Lied?"

"Yeah. You told me I could find a murder witness in that

vacant house. But the only thing inside was drugs and money, Tony."

"Drugs and money. I don't know nothing about no drugs and money."

"Then why was it in the house?"

"I don't know."

"Well, what do you know, Tony?"

Tony said nothing.

Nash shoved him against the wall. "Don't forget, I got a lot of dirt on you."

Tony eyed Nash, then sighed. "Two men came to me. They said to tell anyone asking about that guy who was killed 'bout two weeks ago, off of Oakdale, that a witness was squatting in the house."

"And why would you agree to that?"

"They gave me two bands."

"Two thousand dollars? What'd they look like?"

Tony shook his head. "It was at night, so it was hard to make out, but both were white and kinda stocky. One was sort of bald and had a thick mustache. The other was taller— had a lot of hair on his head and it was messy, but not much on his face."

Nash loosened his grip on Tony. "And you never seen them before?"

"No, that's the truth, I promise."

Nash stared at his informant. Although Tony was a street-hustling squirt, Nash believed him. "Okay," Nash said while completely releasing Tony. "Keep your ear to the ground 'cause I may be back for more information, and you better have something."

Tony adjusted his shirt. "Yeah, sure."

Nash nodded toward the opposite end of the alley.

Tony glanced in that direction before fixing on Nash's face.

Nash shrugged. "Go," he said.

Tony walked down the alley, periodically glancing back at

Nash and Kristi. Ten seconds later, he disappeared into the busyness of the main street.

Nash turned to find Kristi staring at him. "What?" he asked. "You think I'm crazy for chasing him, then lettin' him go?"

She shook her head. "No. It's not that."

"Then what is it?"

"Those men he described…"

"Yeah?"

"I think I know them."

FIVE

"Whatcha mean you think you know them?" Nash asked Kristi as they walked back to the car.

She pursed her lips and stared into the distance as if she were chasing a memory. "I mean, they sound like some men I saw."

"Where?"

"Near Brookhaven."

"What were you doing there?"

"Shopping. As I was leaving the store, I noticed those men standing outside a cafe."

Nash bounced a shoulder. "Okay. What were they doing, talking?" he asked while pressing the keyless entry button to unlock the Acura.

"Yes. With Frank. This was just two days before he was murdered."

"How come you never told me?"

"Didn't seem important until now."

Nash sighed, then gestured for Kristi to enter the car. Once inside, Nash started the car, then turned to Kristi, who sat staring through the passenger side window. "I think you should reconsider leaving town."

She whipped her head toward Nash. "I already told you I'm not leaving."

"Kristi, this is messy, and you're too close to it. Could be very dangerous."

She half smiled. "Well, that's why I have you."

"I'm serious, Kristi. This situation doesn't look good. Your husband's death is somehow tied to missing drugs and money that was seized from some dangerous people."

Kristi shrugged. "Doesn't surprise me."

Nash stared at her.

"Like I told you before," Kristi continued. "I believe he was murdered by cops."

"You think those two men are cops?"

"Don't know."

Nash faced the windshield. "Okay, then," he said while putting the car into gear.

"Where are we going?"

"Shopping."

They drove for twenty minutes before entering Brookhaven. Under Kristi's direction, Nash turned into a parking garage near downtown. They found a parking spot on the first level, then walked to the main street. Multiple three to ten-story buildings flanked them as they stood on the sparsely populated sidewalk.

"So, where did you see them?" Nash asked.

Kristi pointed her thumb across the street. "This way."

They crossed the newly paved road and landed on the opposite sidewalk, then dodged a few pedestrians and swinging shop doors on their way up the sidewalk. Nash trailed as Kristi led the way. A few seconds later, she stopped in front of a window with a large coffee mug decal stickered to the glass.

Kristi hunched her shoulders. "This is where I saw them," she said.

Nash surveyed the area.

"Not sure what you're hoping to find here," Kristi went on.

Nash stared through the window into the cafe. His eyes widened when he noticed certain patrons. He quickly turned his back to the glass.

Kristi squinted. "What is it?" she asked.

Nash nodded toward the window.

Kristi peeped through the window. "Oh, I see," she said, turning to Nash and grinning. "Don't worry, I'm sure they're not looking for you."

"You can't be sure of that. Do any of them look familiar?"

"No."

"Alright."

"So what now?"

Nash sucked in his lips and looked toward the clear blue sky.

"I mean, we don't even know if I saw the same men your mate is talking about," Kristi continued.

"He's not my mate. He's an informant."

"Yeah, you know what I mean."

The cafe's door swung open, and three uniformed officers walked out. Nash turned toward Kristi. He nodded as the men walked past.

"What about them? Are they your mates?" Kristi said.

"Funny."

"This was a waste of a drive."

Nash shook his head, then sighed. "Maybe. Hey, did your husband ever bring you here?"

"What, to this cafe?"

"To this area?"

"He may have come here with me a few times to shop."

"But he didn't come here for business or work?"

Kristi shrugged. "From what I know, most of his business was conducted downtown. But I already told you that like the second day we met, remember?"

Nash did remember. He recalled looking into Frank Jackson's daily routine. Mr. Jackson was a financial adviser for a large hedge fund company in downtown Atlanta. He worked long days, either at the company's downtown location or at his home office.

"Yeah, I remember," Nash said to Kristi. "Just wanted to confirm he didn't have any work clients or other business you were aware of."

"Not that I know of. But obviously something was going on since I saw him here." Kristi exhaled. "So this little trip was a waste."

"Not necessarily."

Kristi's eyebrows furrowed.

"If Frank had no business here, he wouldn't've recommended meeting here," Nash continued.

"Yeah."

"So, more than likely, the two men he met suggested this spot."

"Okay."

"I think those men are cops. Local cops."

"How do you know for sure?"

"I don't," Nash said while glancing at the cafe. "But there may be a way to find out. Let's go."

They crossed the street and walked back to the parking garage. Nash removed his cell phone and turned it on. When the phone came on, several missed calls and messages displayed on the screen. Most of the calls and messages were from Chris. A couple were from Moore. Focusing on the task at hand, Nash ignored the messages and unlocked the car. As he and Kristi settled inside, he asked his phone for directions to the nearest library. The phone provided directions to a location six minutes away. They made it there in five.

"Mind telling me what we're doing here?" Kristi asked as they passed through the library's automatic sliding doors.

"The police department has a repository of police officers and their assigned precincts," Nash said.

"Okay."

"Good afternoon," a lady with salt-and-pepper hair greeted them. "Can I help you?" she continued, adjusting her thick frame glasses.

"Yes, ma'am," Nash said. "Where's your computer lab?"

"Do you have a card with us?"

Nash reached into his back pocket. "I don't, but I am a police officer," he said, flipping his wallet open and exposing his badge. "Here on official law enforcement business."

The lady craned toward the wallet and squinted at the badge. She glanced at Nash, then slowly leaned back until she was once again standing straight.

"It's that way," she said, pointing toward a room near the back of the building.

"Thanks," Nash told her.

Nash and Kristi headed toward the room, dodging a book rack and passing through a row of shelves on their way. Inside, a handful of individuals occupied a few of the computer stations, leaving nearing a dozen open. Nash and Kristi walked to an open station. Nash sat in front of the screen and gestured for Kristi to pull over a chair. She complied while Nash opened the computer's web browser.

Kristi leaned toward Nash's ear. "So I'm guessing you're going to search the repository for those men?" she asked in a whisper.

"That's the idea," Nash whispered while typing in the repository website's URL.

"Sounds like this'll take some time."

Nash shrugged. "We'll see."

He typed in his login credentials and searched for precincts in Brookhaven.

"Okay, not too bad," he said.

"What?"

"There's only two precincts. One with thirty-three officers and the other has forty-one."

"Not too bad."

Nash dragged the mouse and clicked on a link for the first precinct, then another link that took him to a page with the officers' names and pictures. They spent ten minutes going through the images, but none of the officers looked familiar to Kristi.

"Alright then," she said. "Let's try the other location."

Nash clicked through to the second precinct's list of officers' pictures. The first eight didn't ring any bells for Kristi, but on the ninth picture, she squinted and leaned toward the computer screen.

"He looks familiar," she said.

The screen displayed a picture of a stocky man with a buzz cut and a thick mustache.

"Says his name is Jerry Ward," Nash commented. "He matches the description Tony gave."

Kristi nodded. "Yes. I definitely remember seeing him."

"Good. Let's see if we can find his friend."

They continued through the list, but none of the officers looked familiar to Kristi or matched Tony's description.

"Well," Nash said, "we got one name, so I guess this trip wasn't a complete bust."

Kristi cocked her head to the side. "I guess not. So what now?"

Nash glanced at her, and before a thought could enter his mind, his phone buzzed. As Nash fumbled his phone from his pocket. The individuals at the other computer stations turned in their chairs and glared at him.

Nash shrugged. "Sorry," he said as he silenced the phone.

The phone displayed Chris's name.

"Who is it?" Kristi asked.

"A colleague."

Kristi winced. "Can you trust them?"

Nash bounced a shoulder. "I hope so. C'mon, let's get out of here."

They left the library. On their way to the car, Nash returned Chris's call.

"Yo, Derrick, where you at?" Chris answered. "Been tryna call you."

"I know. Lot's going on."

"Barnhill was shot last night, and you're a suspect. What happened?"

Nash sighed. Kristi stopped at the passenger-side door and looked at him.

"We were ambushed," Nash spoke into the phone. "He believed me. Offered to take me home. And on the way to his car, they shot him."

"Who?" Chris asked.

"Don't know, but I'm gonna find out."

"Look, man. You hafta turn yourself in."

"How's Barnhill?"

"He's gonna make it."

"Does he have a security detail?"

"Yeah, I'm here with him now at Piedmont."

Nash nodded at the phone. "Good. Is he conscious?"

"Not yet. Resting."

"Okay. Don't leave him alone with anyone you don't trust."

"Got it. You gonna turn yourself in?"

"Yeah, eventually. Hey, does the name Jerry Ward ring any bells?"

"Nah. Why?"

"Can you have one of the guys you trust at the station dig into him?"

"Sure, what am I looking for?"

"Anything. He's a cop."

"For real? This sounds serious," Chris said.

Nash again nodded at the phone. "Yeah."

"If they ask me if I heard from—"

"You tell the truth. But be careful. They can't think you believe me. And I won't be answering anymore of your calls."

"Yo, wait," Chris said as Nash ended the call.

Nash understood that the less Chris knew, the safer the big guy would be. And he knew of other ways to reach him if needed. But Chris's easy accessibility to Nash could implicate him, since Nash was a suspect and all.

"That's your work colleague?" Kristi asked as Nash unlocked the car door.

He nodded.

"What happened?"

"Nothing. Just asked him to look into Ward."

"You trust him?"

"Who, Big C?"

"Big C?"

"Yeah, that's his nickname growing up. Known him for years. So yeah, I do trust him."

"Okay, then," Kristi said while opening her door.

"Give me a minute. I need to make another call."

Kristi's eyebrows furrowed as she entered the car. Nash turned his back to the car and dialed Moore's number.

"Officer Nash," Moore answered. "Been looking for you."

"I figured."

"You know why?"

Nash said nothing.

"Let me help you," Moore continued. "Less than eight hours after finding you with drugs and money missing from evidence, you're no longer in jail, and Lieutenant Barnhill is shot."

"He let me go, and I didn't shoot him."

Nash glanced at the car and saw Kristi staring at him through the windshield.

"Okay, come to the station and we can talk about it," Moore said.

"Too dangerous. Like I told you when you arrested me, it was a setup. Not sure who can be trusted."

"Then who wounded Lieutenant Barnhill?"

"Not sure. But there were two men."

"Why should I believe you?"

"It's the truth."

The line went silent.

After a long moment, Moore sighed. "I tell you what," he said. "Let's meet."

"Okay. But just you."

"You have my word. Where would you like to meet?"

"The Omni. Across the street from the State Farm Are—"

"I know the place," Moore interrupted.

"Good. Be in the lobby in an hour. I'll call you then." Nash ended the call.

SIX

The Omni was a five-star hotel situated downtown, across the street from the State Farm Arena. The sky-rise hotel boasted a lot of large windows and clean lines. There wasn't much traffic on the main entrance road to the hotel, which made sense considering it was late afternoon in the middle of the week. On the drive there, Nash tried convincing Kristi to stay at the motel while he went to the meet. Of course, she wasn't having it and insisted on participating.

"Make sure you stick to the plan," Nash told her as he found a parking spot off the main road, two blocks across the street from the hotel's front entrance. "Just go inside and sit in the lobby. Keep your distance—don't won't him recognizing you."

"Got it," Kristi said.

"He should be alone. Text me when you see him. He usually wears—"

"Simmer down, will you? I've seen him before," Kristi interrupted. "And if he did notice me, it'd be a doddle for me to blag my way out. More difficult for you, innit?"

"Whatever. He should be here in about twenty minutes, if not already. If anything looks off, just get outta there. Okay?"

"Okay," Kristi said before exiting the car.

Nash tracked her as she circled the hood, then crossed the street, headed toward the hotel's front entrance. As she walked through the front door, Nash looked at his phone. The clock suggested Moore would be in the lobby within the next seventeen minutes. Nash adjusted in his chair and watched the hotel's entrance for eight minutes. A few cars passed along the main street and entered in and out of the parking garage as he waited. He checked his phone. There were no messages from Kristi. The rear of a police cruiser caught Nash's eye.

The vehicle eased to the curb near the hotel's entrance and parked. An officer emerged from the car. Nash's mouth gaped when he recognized the officer. It was the receptionist officer from the night before. As the bald, thick-bearded man made his way to the entrance, Nash stared at him through squinted eyes. Nash's phone buzzed.

He's here, displayed the text from Kristi.

Nash ejected his gun's magazine and inspected it before reinserting it, then pulled back the slide. After emerging from the car, he placed the pistol in his front waistband and concealed it behind his shirt. He then hurried toward the hotel, nearly stumbling as he raced across the street.

Nash darted inside, parting a family of four standing in the foyer on his way to the lobby. He immediately noticed Kristi sitting to his right at a high table near a bar. She stood when she saw him and nodded toward the center of the lobby. Nash followed her nod and saw Moore standing by the check-in counter. The detective wore his usual blue jeans and blazer arrangement. The receptionist officer approached him. Moore's thick mustache and equally thick eyebrows furrowed as he shrugged his mouth and squinted at the sight of the officer.

Nash waved Kristi over. She dodged around the table, and the two hurried out the front door.

"Who's that policeman?" Kristi asked on their way to the car.

"Not exactly sure," Nash answered. "A new hire at my precinct."

They waited in the Acura for three minutes before the receptionist officer exited the hotel, got in his car, and pulled off.

Nash removed his phone and dialed Moore.

"You're here?" he answered.

"I thought I said to come alone."

"I did."

"Why was that uniform with you?"

"He wasn't with me. I believe he may have... um... followed me."

"Who is he? What's his name?"

"Don't know. He works the night shift—only seen him a couple of times. Don't know his name."

"You just saw him. What's on his nameplate?"

The line went silent briefly.

"I didn't catch it."

"Right. And you're a detective."

"I'm telling you, he must've followed me. I was shocked to see him here."

"What did he say to you?"

"Just that he was in the area grabbing a bite and he saw me in the lobby and wanted to say hi."

Nash scoffed. "You don't find that strange?" he asked Moore before glancing at Kristi in the passenger seat.

"Very," Moore answered. "And trust me, I plan to look into it, but first things first."

"I'll see you in a few minutes." Nash ended the call and turned to Kristi. "I'm going back in. Shouldn't be long. Can you wait here? I don't want him seeing us together."

Kristi bounced a shoulder. "Makes sense."

A bit surprised he wasn't met with resistance, Nash

nodded, then exited the car and made the short walk back to the hotel.

In the lobby, Moore sat at a table near the same bar as Kristi had just minutes before. He kept his eyes on the entrance and noticed when Nash walked in. With his head on a swivel, Nash walked to the table and sat across from him.

Moore shrugged. "Let's talk."

"Like I've been telling you. I was set up," Nash said.

"Yeah. But you never told me why you were in that house," Moore said. "So I'll ask again. Why were you there?"

Nash sighed but said nothing.

"Okay. I guess this was a waste of time for both of us."

"Like I said, I was set up. So I'll tell you why I was there when you tell me why you were there."

"Fair enough. I received an *anonymous* tip."

"That's convenient."

"It's the truth," Moore said, staring directly into Nash's eyes. "Your turn."

"Fine. I was looking into one of your cases."

"What?"

"Yeah. The Frank Jackson case."

"Why you snooping around my case?"

"Thought I'd log some detective hours. But seems I was getting too close, and someone didn't like it."

Moore grabbed his chin and glanced at the table. "I've been on this case, and no one's come after me."

Nash stared at Moore but said nothing.

"What's that look?" Moore said. He leaned toward Nash. "You think I had something to do with setting you up?"

"I'm not saying that."

"Tell that to the look on your face."

Nash shook his head. "Maybe they plan on coming after you. Just haven't yet."

Moore raised a brow.

"Does the name Jerry Ward sound familiar?"

"No, should it?"

"Maybe not. You have any suspects in Jackson's murder?"

"There are some persons of interest."

Nash fixed on Moore's face, waiting for him to elaborate.

"But you know I can't share that with you," Moore continued. "Given the current circumstances and all."

"Of course not."

"So what now?"

"I'm gonna find out who framed me."

"How do you plan on doing that?"

"I'll let you know when I figure it out." Nash stood, and as he pivoted away from the table, Moore stood.

"Officer Nash," he said. "I'm gonna do some digging of my own. If I find anything conflicting with what you told me—"

"It'd be false, cause I told you the truth," Nash interrupted before continuing toward the front entrance.

On his way outside, Nash wondered if he could trust Moore. The detective appeared honest, but Nash felt hesitant to trust anyone with the PD. And when he looked in the Acura's direction, he was reminded why.

The receptionist officer's squad car sat parked behind the Acura. The officer stood outside his car, but he wasn't alone. Nash's eyes widened as the officer grabbed a kicking and screaming Kristi in a bear hug, then forced her into the back of the cruiser.

Nash raced across the street. "Kristi!"

When he was within ten yards of the car, the vehicle sped off, leaving a cloud of smoke and the stench of burnt rubber and exhaust in its path.

SEVEN

Nash rushed back to the hotel lobby. Moore was no longer at the table. Nash circled the lobby and checked the bathroom but still found no sign of the detective. Nash's heart pounded in his chest, and his breathing became heavy. He sat at a table while catching his breath.

After a few moments, his heart rate slowed, and his breathing regulated. Another moment passed before an idea hit him. He dialed Chris.

"Hi. What's up?" Chris answered.

"Hey, do you know that new receptionist officer?"

"Uh—I mean—I know of him."

"What's his name?"

"I think it's Fletcher. Kevin Fletcher. Why?"

"I need a favor, fast. Don't ask," Nash said while standing and making his way to the door.

"Sure. What is it?"

"I need to track and locate his squad car."

The line went silent briefly. "Uh—wh—"

"Don't ask."

Another bout of silence. "Okay. Give me a few minutes," Chris said.

"Thanks. It's an emergency."

"Alright. I'm on it."

Nash ended the call, then headed to the car. He waited behind the wheel for three minutes before his phone rang.

"Yep," he answered.

"I found him," Chris said. "His squad car, at least."

"Good. Where?"

"Looks like he's parked near an alley by the aquarium."

"That's just on the other side of Olympic Park. You sure?"

"It's what I'm showing."

"Thanks."

Nash ended the call, then started the Acura and floored the car all the way to the aquarium. Three minutes later, he was cruising along the building's perimeter. It didn't take him long to spot the patrol car angled toward the alley like it was stolen by a group of teenagers who went for a joyride before ditching it. Nash eased the Acura behind the squad car and parked. He stepped out and immediately trained his gun on the police cruiser. Circling around the passenger side, he noticed the inside was empty. Nash lowered his gun and surveyed the alley.

Near the end of the alley, a skinny man with an apron sat leaned against the wall across from a dumpster. Nash rushed toward the man. He dodged around a stuffed garbage bag as he approached the fella.

"Imma cop. You okay?" he asked the skinny man.

The man raised his head and looked at Nash through squinted blue eyes. "Was bringing out the trash and got shoved into the wall."

Nash knelt and saw a lump on the side of the man's head.

"A bald cop chasing some woman," the skinny fella continued. He pointed his thumb at the ajar door. "They went inside."

"Okay, stay here until help comes," Nash said while standing.

He peeked through the door's slit. A man and woman wearing aprons similar to the skinny man's stood near a commercial grill talking. Nash pulled the door open, then hurried inside. The man and woman winced at the sight of Nash entering the kitchen.

"Gun," the woman said in a low tone. Almost as if she was out of breath.

"No, no, it's okay. Imma cop." Nash scanned the area. "Did you see a woman and a uniformed police officer come through?"

Both the man and woman nodded and pointed toward a pair of swinging doors near the front of the kitchen.

"Thanks," Nash said. "Call 9-1-1. Tell them to send an ambulance for your friend outside," he said on his way to the doors.

On the opposite side of the doors, there was a counter with two registers on top. Beyond the counter, individuals roamed about exploring the many exhibits surrounding the aquarium's expansive open floor. Nash stuffed his gun in his front waistband and pulled his shirt down over it. With his head on a swivel, he stepped onto the floor. Various aquatic displays and wildlife skeletal systems flanked him as he followed a group around a large tank filled with fish.

Nash stopped walking and stood at the center of the floor. Uncertain where to go, he pivoted left, then right. His neck rotated, and his eyes searched. And just when a feeling of hopelessness encroached upon his mind, he noticed something. Two aquarium employees knelt by a small, toppled, broken display. The employees found their footing amidst the shattered glass and water, then worked together to stand the display upright. Beyond the mess was a hallway. Nash made his way in that direction.

"Hold on, sir," one employee said to him. "We have to block this area off until we get this cleaned up."

"Don't worry about it," Nash told him while flashing his badge. "Imma cop."

The employees watched with gaping mouths as Nash stepped around the broken glass. In the hallway, a decision awaited him. Three doors. One on the wall to his right and two on the left. The door on the left, nearest to the end of the hall, was ajar. Nash saw it and ignored the other doors and his training. Per the academy, he should clear the doors closest to the front first. But Nash followed his instincts and went straight to the half-opened door. After removing his gun, he trained it in the door's direction.

When he was five feet away, faint footsteps and droning flowed from the door. Nash quickly covered the remaining five feet, then pulled the door completely open. He entered a huge pump room. Pipes, large and small, ran vertically up the walls and horizontally across the ceiling. The water pumps hummed as rushing water moved through the pipes. On the concrete floor, yellow tape outlined the hazard-free or recommended path. Nash followed it to a large pump, where he heard more obscure footsteps knock against the floor. Peeking around the pump, he saw Kristi running toward the opposite end of the room. The receptionist officer, who Nash now knew as Kevin Fletcher, dashed after her.

Nash turned the corner and raced after them. He passed more pipes, pumps, and large reservoir tanks as he closed the distance. Breathing in the scent of machine oil and sulfur with each stride, he slowed to round another corner. Fletcher chased Kristi up a flight of steps. Nash rushed after them. He cleared four risers before Fletcher acknowledged the aluminum steps clanking behind him. The receptionist officer stepped onto the landing, then pivoted toward Nash, charging at him. As Fletcher brought his gun to bear, Nash shoulder-butted him. Fletcher fell to the floor and dropped his gun. Nash loomed over him with his own gun trained on the now unarmed man. Kristi noticed and stopped running.

"Don't move," Nash told Fletcher.

Fletcher turned to Nash. With heavy breaths, he stared at the gun, then at Nash's face.

"Who's working with you, Fletcher?" Nash asked.

The bald man smirked but didn't say anything.

Nash stepped closer to him. "You betta start talking."

Kristi approached. Nash glanced at her.

"You okay?" he asked.

She nodded. "Yeah. I'm fine."

Nash kicked Fletcher's leg. "Start talking now!"

"Why would I be working with someone?" Fletcher said.

"Maybe for the same reason you kidnapped her."

Fletcher grimaced.

"So, there's you and Ward," Nash continued. "Who else is involved in this mess?"

Fletcher glanced at the floor. "I don't know what you're talking about."

Kristi stepped to him. "What do you know about my husband's murder?"

Fletcher chuckled.

"You think that's funny?" Kristi arched down and reached for Fletcher.

Nash scooted between them. "Hey, wait!"

Seizing the opportunity, Fletcher crawled to his feet and wrapped his arms around Nash's waist, grabbing him in a tackle. Kristi yelped as the two men stumbled past her. Nash's back smacked into a metal rail. He quickly shifted his stance, then kneed Fletcher in the gut. The bald man groaned while loosening his hold. On pure instinct, Nash flipped his pistol and gripped its barrel. He axed the butt of the gun into the back of Fletcher's skull. The bald man dropped, rattling the aluminum floor as his body sprawled across it.

"You okay?" Kristi asked as she approached Nash.

"I'm fine," Nash said. He pointed at Fletcher. "He's gonna be out for a minute."

Nash knelt and frisked the unconscious man. From his front pants pocket, he fished out a flip phone.

"What is it?" Kristi asked.

"A phone," Nash said before placing the device inside his own pocket.

Nash lifted Fletcher's upper body from the floor before dragging the officer toward the railing. Halfway there, Nash's lower back and calf muscles were telling him Fletcher should probably diet. Nash laid the unconscious man on the floor next to the railing. After removing the officer's handcuffs from the case on his belt, Nash grabbed Fletcher's hand and cuffed him to the rail.

"When he wakes, we can get some answers," Kristi said.

Nash shook his head. "No, we should get outta here. The cops are on their way," he said before grabbing Kristi's hand.

She glanced at him and forced a smile. They hustled down the steps, then raced through the aquarium before exiting the same way Nash had entered. The two continued holding hands until they were halfway down the alley. They looked at each other and let go. Nothing forced, just a natural, gentle release. They continued on to the street. After circling Fletcher's squad car, they hustled toward the Acura. Nash made his way to the driver's side and Kristi to the passenger's. Just when Nash opened the door, his phone rang. The screen showed Chris's number.

"What's up, Chris?" Nash answered as he and Kristi entered the car.

"Hi," he said, nearly out of breath. "Just wanted to let you know Barnhill is conscious."

Nash started the car. "Good. You there with him?"

"No, on my way there now."

"Me too."

"Think that's a good idea?"

"I'll be careful." Nash put the car in gear. "Call you when I'm there."

"Aight."

"Hey," Nash said while veering the car onto the street. "Fletcher's at the aquarium."

"Huh?"

Nash glanced at Kristi. "He's involved in all of this. I left him handcuffed in the pump room."

"What? At the aquarium?"

"Yeah. He's dirty."

"Okay. I—I'll try to have him held, I guess."

"Thanks." Nash ended the call before making a left turn, then placing his attention on Kristi.

She stared at the windshield.

"You okay?" he asked her.

"Yeah. Just a little shook. I'm sorry. I was standing outside the car when he grabbed me."

"You don't hafta apologize. Just glad you're safe."

"Made such a fuss in the back, he pulled over and threatened to tase me," Kristi continued, seemingly ignoring Nash's previous comment.

Nash listened, sharing his gaze between her and the road.

"But when he opened the door, I kicked him in an area he probably doesn't use much, then climbed out of the car and ran." She looked at Nash. "I was happy to see you. Thank you."

"Of course." Nash chuckled while turning his attention to the road. "In an area he probably doesn't use much."

Kristi sniggered.

EIGHT

They made it to Piedmont Atlanta Hospital in under twenty minutes. It was a ten-story brick structure situated outside the heart of Atlanta. The building had a unique shape. If you were to take the helicopter on the roof up, the building would look like a large L from the sky. A parking garage was at the end of the L's short line. Nash found a spot inside, then killed the Acura's engine.

"Need to go in and check on my lieutenant," he told Kristi.

"Got it. And you need me to stay in the car," Kristi said.

"No, I actually want you to come in with me."

Kristi winced. "Really?"

"Yeah, really. With what just happened—we just need to be careful when we get inside."

Kristi gave Nash a closed-lip smile. "Okay," she said.

Nash dialed Chris and found he was already inside the hospital. Chris gave Nash Barnhill's room number.

Nash ended the call. "Room 619," he said to Kristi.

They exited the car and took the parking garage elevator to the hospital's main lobby. Passing through the sparsely populated lobby, they arrived at the main elevators uninterrupted. There was a security guard, but he was occupied chatting to a woman with her arm in a sling near the front entrance. Nash and Kristi rode the elevator to the sixth floor and found room 619. A uniformed officer stood outside the room.

"Wait here," Nash instructed Kristi.

She stopped near the nurse's station and watched as Nash continued toward the room. When he was seven feet away, the officer lifted his small palm at him.

"Hold it there," he said.

Nash paused and stared into the green eyes of the freckled-faced officer. The officer parted his lips to speak, but before he could say anything, Chris exited the room.

"He's okay," he told the freckled-faced officer. Chris waved Nash into the room.

Nash glanced back at Kristi. She forced a smile and gave him a gentle nod. Nash returned the nod, then followed his paunchy friend into the room. The beeps from an EKG monitor welcomed Nash as he made his way to Barnhill's bedside. The lieutenant's afro draped wet down his forehead. His facial complexion paled just a shade darker than the spots of gray in his hair and goatee. He looked weak, but his eyes were full and lively.

"Hi there, Lieutenant," Nash said.

"Derrick," Barnhill said in his usual serious tone. "It's good to see you're okay."

Nash patted his shoulder. "And it's good to see you're getting better."

"Please tell me you got the shooter."

Nash shook his head. "There were two. They got away."

Barnhill glanced at the foot of his bed. "I was telling Chris we were ambushed but didn't know by who or how many." He shared his gaze between Nash and Chris. "Do we know who they are?"

Chris hunched his shoulders and looked at Nash.

"Not a hundred percent sure. But I believe some cops are involved," Nash said.

Barnhill raised a brow. "Makes sense. The money and drugs you were found with didn't get there by themselves."

"Exactly. This seems to be tied to the Jackson murder, too."

Barnhill nodded. "You have any evidence?"

Nash walked to the door and beckoned Kristi with a wave. Her eyebrows knitted, and she hesitated before joining the three men inside the room.

Nash closed the door, then stood next to her at the center of the room. "This is Mrs. Jackson. Frank Jackson's wife," he announced.

Chris and Barnhill listened as Nash explained how he had been working with Kristi to investigate Frank Jackson's murder and all the events from when Barnhill was shot leading up to the hospital visit.

"What's the cop's name?" Barnhill asked.

"Fletcher," Nash said.

Barnhill squinted and gently shook his head. "No, he works the front desk at our precinct. The other name you mentioned. Barry Boyd, Larry Warren."

Chris's phone rang. Everyone paused and looked as he glanced at the screen.

"It's from the station," he announced. "I betta take it," he continued on his way out of the room.

Nash turned back to Barnhill. The lieutenant's face oozed with fatigue.

"That was Jerry Ward," he said.

"Yeah, that's it. I know him. He's with some precinct on the west side." Barnhill yawned.

Kristi glanced at Nash as to say, *maybe we should let him rest*. He gave her a gesture that suggested he understood.

"I remember he had a partner," Barnhill continued. "Can't remember his name right now, but he's no longer on the force. He prob—"

"I tell you what, Lieutenant," Nash interrupted. "We'll pick up on this later."

The door opened, and Chris entered. "That was my guy at the station," he said, stuffing the phone inside his pocket, then shutting the door. "They got Fletcher there. I told them to hold him."

"I should get down there," Nash said.

"Sure that's a good idea? Moore—"

"I'm not worried about Moore. I had a talk with him earlier. If he can't see I was framed, he's not much of a detective. Fletcher is the only one who can tell us who's involved with this mess."

Chris shook his head and grinned. "Maybe not."

"What?"

A long, rhythmic grunt cut through the air. Everyone's eyes followed the noise to Barnhill's bed. The lieutenant was sound asleep and snoring.

Kristi sighed, then turned to Nash. "I'll be outside," she said before making her way toward the door.

"Guess we should finish talking outside," Chris said to Nash.

The men followed Kristi into the hall. She continued to the nurse's station while Nash and Chris stood just outside of the room.

"Fletcher," Nash said. "I want to speak with him."

Chris pointed his palms at Nash. "Chill for a sec," he said. "My guy looked into Jerry Ward, and like you said, he's a cop."

"Yeah. Barnhill said he knew him. Said he had a partner that's no longer with the force."

Chris bounced a shoulder. "Haven't found anything about his partners, but I know where Ward is."

Nash's eyes widened. "Where?"

Another grin crossed Chris's face. "You not gonna believe it."

NINE

Nash followed Chris to the elevators, with Kristi trailing behind them a few paces. Chris pressed the down arrow, and a few seconds later, the elevator door dinged, then slid open. The group crowded into the car. Chris pressed the button with the big five on it. The button lit up, the elevator door thumped closed, and the car hummed into motion. Moments later, they filed out of the elevator and onto the fifth floor. The floor was practically empty, with only a few nurses roaming the halls.

Chris craned toward a sign on the wall. "Room 512," he murmured to himself.

The room was near the center of the hall, diagonally across from the nurse's station. Voices drifted from the room. Chris walked inside first, Nash followed, but Kristi stayed in the hall. A nurse sporting red hair in a bobbed cut stood over the bed with her back to the door.

"You can't leave," she said, struggling to keep the patient in the bed. "You haven't been discharged yet, sir."

"Imma cop," the man in the bed protested. His gown rose, revealing his hairy legs as he continued to scuffle with the nurse. "You can't do this to me."

When the man noticed Chris, he paused his fight with the nurse and stared. And when he saw Nash, his mouth gaped. Nash immediately recognized the man. Jerry Ward. He looked the same as he did in the repository, except he had a little more hair on his head and his mustache was unkempt. Nash made note of the bandages wrapped around Ward's left shoulder.

"Ma'am, we have a few questions for him," Chris told the nurse.

She looked him up and down. "Officer, he just got out of surgery a few hours ago. He's a bit weak and needs to take his pain meds before the morphine wears off."

"It won't take long," Nash said. "And we promise he'll take his medicine afterwards."

The nurse shared her gaze between Nash and Chris before cocking her head to the side. "Well, he seems to have settled down now, so I'll give you five minutes," she said before leaving the room.

"Should be plenty of time," Nash said, turning his attention to Ward.

"What do you want?" Ward asked.

Chris reached to his duty belt and removed his cuffs. He grabbed Ward's right hand and cuffed it to the bed rail.

"What's this?" Ward protested. "Imma cop too."

"Not for long," Nash said.

Ward glanced at Nash, then rolled his eyes and glanced away. "Who are you?" he asked.

"Tryna play stupid, huh?" Nash said. He stepped to the bedside. "You know who I am."

"Do I?"

"You and your partner tried to set me up."

"Really?"

"Yeah. And then you shot at me and my lieutenant."

Ward looked at Nash. "You have no evidence for any of this. So stop harassing me."

"Why'd you try to frame me?"

"I don't know what you're talking about," Ward said while moving his sights to an empty spot on the wall.

Nash craned toward the injured man. "That looks like a nasty wound," he said. "What was it, a gunshot?"

Ward said nothing. Nash reached for the damaged shoulder.

"Derrick, take it easy, man," Chris said.

Ward flinched. "Hey, what are you doing?"

"Getting answers," Nash said while gently resting his hand on Ward's shoulder.

"Like I said—aah."

Nash squeezed the injured shoulder. Ward snarled, exposing small, stained teeth under his bushy mustache.

"I said I don't know what you're—aaaah!"

"I'm not playin' with you."

"Yo, Derrick, chill out, man," Chris admonished.

"Not until he tells me the truth."

Nash squeezed harder, and Ward went from hollering to squirming in the bed. Kristi peeked inside. Her eyebrows knitted as she locked eyes with Nash. He gave her a dismissal wave. Not to dispel her, but to assure her there was nothing to worry about. She scanned the room briefly before shaking her head and ducking back into the hall.

"You sure you don't know what I'm talking about? You and your partner shot at me, remember?"

"Okay, okay," Ward grunted under the pain.

Nash let up, but kept his hand on Ward's shoulder. "What's your friend's name?"

"Patrick Dent. And he ain't my friend."

"I thought you two were partners."

"That doesn't make him my friend, does it? He's not even a cop anymore."

"Why'd'chu come after me?"

"You were getting too close, alright."

"Too close to what?"

Ward shook his head but said nothing. Nash pressed.

"Oww—wait! As a fellow brother in blue, I can't tell you that. They'll kill me."

Nash furrowed his eyebrows and shrugged his lips. "You tried to kill me, but now we're brothers?"

"I'd tell you if I could. I swear."

"Yeah, right," Chris huffed.

"Same thing I was thinking," Nash told Chris before squeezing Ward's shoulder.

"Aah! Please," the wounded man pleaded.

"Hey, D, that's enough," Chris said. "At what point are we like them?"

"What's going on here?" the nurse asserted as she entered the room.

Nash released his grip and shoved Ward's shoulder. "Nothing," he told her. "I think he's ready for those pain meds now." Nash brushed past the nurse on his way to the door. "You okay?" he asked Kristi when he entered the hall.

"I'm fine. You? Things got a little dicey in there, I see."

"He wasn't cooperating, is all."

Kristi forced a smile.

"Did you get a look at his face?"

She nodded.

"You saw him with your husband in Brookhaven that day?"

"I'm positive he was one of them."

"Okay."

"Yo, Derrick." Chris exited the room with his arms open and shoulders hunched. "Bro, what was that?"

"Just tryin' to get some answers," Nash said. "But you heard him admit to framing me, right?"

"Yeah, I heard him. I'll keep him under arrest and get someone to watch him."

Chris's phone rang. He glanced at the screen, then at Nash, before shaking his head.

"Chris speaking," he answered. After listening for a moment, he frowned. "Yeah, I understand, but—" Chris looked at Nash and again shook his head before turning and walking down the hall. "He was framed," he said as his voice slowly faded into the hallway walls.

"Wonder what that's about," Kristi said.

Nash sighed. "I'm sure he'll let us know." He cupped his chin as a thought came to him. "We need to visit your husband's office."

"Why?"

"Something's missing. I wanna poke around."

"You know the company won't let us do that. Frank worked with a lot of confidential financial documents."

"No, no. Not his work office. The home office at your house."

"Oh. Sure. But your pal Detective Moore may already have anything of use."

"But he could've missed something."

"He came to the house with two other officers a day after I met you." Kristi shook her head. "Not sure why it took them nearly a week to begin Frank's investigation, but it made me even more suspicious of the cops. That's why I was at the station when we met. Wanted an update on the investigation."

Nash nodded. "I remember you telling me. The gears move slow at the precinct, and they probably wanted to give you a few days to handle Frank's arrangements. The PD's not all bad."

Kristi glanced at the floor.

"But I still wanna check out the office again," Nash continued.

Kristi shrugged. "Sure."

Chris returned with his phone in hand. He looked at

Nash, his face twisted with uncertainty. "That was Moore," he said while placing the phone inside his pocket.

"Naw," Nash responded sarcastically.

"Hey, he's heated with you."

"Naw," Nash repeated with the same tone.

Chris scoffed. "He's upset about the incident with Fletcher at the aquarium."

"I'm sure he is. You told him I was framed?"

"Yeah. I told him about Ward and Dent too, but he said neither of us is a detective, and this is his investigation, so he'll look at the evidence and come to his own conclusion."

"That sounds 'bout right."

"And you know he's expecting you at the station."

Nash sighed. "Yeah."

"I told him you'll probably swing by since you want to speak with Fletcher and everything. He didn't say anything, so I guess he's okay with it."

Nash shook his head. "I'm getting outta here," he said. "Hafta make a stop before dealing with Moore."

"Alright. I'll hang around here for a bit."

Nash and Kristi walked to the elevator and took it down to the parking garage.

TEN

After ten minutes of driving, they arrived in Buckhead. Kristi was behind the wheel while Nash sat in the passenger seat with his head tilted back and his chin raised. Kristi turned onto a private road where two red-brick walls on either side welcomed them. They approached a security hut, and Kristi stopped the car inches from the boom gate.

A guard exited the hut and waved. "Evening, Mrs. Jackson," he greeted.

"Hi, Joseph," Kristi said.

The guard went back inside. A moment later, the boom gate's arm lifted and Kristi passed through. The Acura droned ahead as tulip poplar trees with light-green, pointy lobe leaves rolled past. Custom luxury homes of various sizes and well-manicured yards soon replaced the trees.

Kristi veered onto another street, then glanced at Nash. "You okay?" she asked.

"Yeah, I'm good," Nash quickly replied.

Kristi shrugged behind the wheel before placing her attention back on the road.

Near the end of the street sat a two-story house with straight lines. The home had larger windows than its neighboring structures. It was slightly smaller than most of the other homes, but it was clean-cut and modern. A tall, black, aluminum horizontal slat fence surrounded the home. Kristi eased the Acura up to the gate and pressed a button on the car's overhead panel. The gate door slid open, and she drove through. They continued up the short driveway before Kristi reached above and pressed another button on the overhead panel. The garage door rose.

They parked the car and entered the house through the kitchen. Kristi disarmed the alarm, then offered Nash something to drink. He declined.

"I'll be in the office," he told her.

Nash walked through the dark house. He remembered that the office was on the first floor. The house had twice the space of his townhome, so he was a bit off-course initially, but his memory quickly refreshed, and it led him straight there. He flicked on the light switch. A faint hum emitted from above, and white LED light from the O-shaped ceiling lamp dispelled the darkness from the room. Nash hurried across the hardwood floor, then onto a soft, tightly woven silk rug where Frank Jackson's desk sat. He rolled the executive leather chair from behind the desk and opened the center drawer. Inside, he found only pens and papers with charts and report summaries. The drawers to the left and right of the desk had folders with more of the same.

Nash stood back from the desk and surveyed the office. Two scenic pictures hung on the wall to his left, and another picture on the wall to his right. Next to the picture on the right was a filing cabinet. Nothing was in the top drawer of the filing cabinet. The second drawer contained blank papers and empty folders. The third and fourth drawers were more of the same.

Nash scoffed. "I guess Kristi wasn't joking about Moore taking everything," he muttered to himself before kneeling and opening the fifth and final drawer.

Empty.

Nash wasn't surprised, but a fume of disappointment wafted from his stomach, to his chest, then out of his mouth as a sigh. When he went to close the drawer, he noticed a small, shiny object resting under the drawer. A silver piece, which would've been easy to miss if the drawer had more contents inside. Nash closed the drawer, stood, then lifted and moved the cabinet a few feet to the left. A small key lay on the floor. He picked up the key before inspecting it, then placed it in his pocket.

Nash moved the filing cabinet back before scanning the office, hoping to find what the key opened. He noticed one picture on the opposite wall hanging slightly off center. Nash cocked his head to the side as he strolled toward the piece of art. He removed the picture, exposing a small square wall safe with a keypad lock.

"What are you doing?" Kristi asked as she entered the room, carrying a water bottle in each hand.

"There's a safe," Nash said while resting the picture on the floor and leaning it against the wall.

"Yeah. I know."

"You didn't tell me last time I was here."

Kristi shrugged. "Didn't think it was important." She shook a bottle at Nash before placing it on the office desk. "Just in case you change your mind and fancy a drink."

"Why didn't you tell me?" Nash asked.

Kristi shrugged again. "Like I said, I didn't think it was a big deal." She walked toward him. "There was nothing inside it. Moore checked it and didn't find anything."

"Could've been something in there before he checked. How long did you know about this safe?"

"I have known about it since Frank and I first moved here. We were planning on using it to store some extra cash and important documents or whatnot."

"Was anything ever inside?"

Kristi's eyebrows knitted, and she gently shook her head. "Not that I know of."

"What's the code?" Nash asked.

"4-8-1-2-7."

Nash pressed the numbers on the keypad, and the safe's locking mechanism thumped. He opened the door and looked inside. The safe's interior was lined with a black carpet material.

"See," Kristi said. "Like I said, empty."

Nash sighed.

"Okay," Kristi continued. "I'm going upstairs to freshen up. Haven't had a proper bath in over twenty-four hours." She tossed the bottle of water between her hands as she pivoted toward the door. "Maybe you should wash up, too. I put some fresh linen and deodorant in the bathroom down the hall. Then afterwards maybe we can grab a late lunch before heading to the police station. Turn off the lights when you're done in here."

Nash watched until she disappeared into the hall. He glanced at the safe's interior and noticed a small slit in the lining material at the bottom. Nash put his index finger between the slit and felt a circular groove beneath the fabric. Peeling the material back, he uncovered a keyhole. Nash removed the key he found under the filing cabinet and inserted it into the keyhole. A grin crossed his face as he turned the key and opened the compartment's door. He removed an envelope and unfolded it. Inside was a sheet of paper.

You work for us now.

Short, but possibly the longest letter the recipient ever read. Nash laid the letter on the safe floor and reached back inside the folder where he found a photo. The picture showed Frank Jackson lying in a bed bare-chested. And he wasn't alone. There was a woman lying next to him.

ELEVEN

"That ain't Kristi," Nash uttered to himself.

The woman in the photo had straight-black shoulder-length hair. A stark contrast to Kristi's natural twisted bobbed cut. Not to mention Kristi's skin was a dark almond complexion. This woman's complexion favored that of honey. Inside the envelope, there were more photos of Frank Jackson with the mystery woman. One showing the two laughing over a meal and another displaying the couple sharing a kiss.

Nash glanced over his shoulder at the door before placing everything back inside the envelope, then folding it and stuffing it into his pocket. He closed the safe and returned the picture to the wall before tossing the small key inside a desk drawer. On his way to the hall, Nash grabbed the bottle of water from the desk and turned off the lights.

He followed Kristi's recommendation and washed up. Once he finished, he went to the living room and sat on the sofa. It wasn't long before footsteps knocked upon the stair's treads and Kristi entered the living room.

"Ready to go?" she asked.

Nash didn't answer.

Kristi craned toward him. "Hey, you alright?"

"Yeah, yeah," Nash said.

"You sure?"

"Were you and Frank having problems?"

Kristi stood straight and winced. "Why you ask that?"

Nash shrugged. "I never asked before and was just wondering."

Kristi squinted. "Well," she breathed out as she sat on the couch next to him. "Moore did ask me. And like I told him—Frank and I didn't have a perfect marriage, but I loved him. And I know he loved me. So, if you're—"

"Kristi, I'm just tryna gather all the facts."

"Here's some facts," Kristi said, a slight crack in her voice. "I loved my husband, and he was killed—taken away from me."

Nash opened his mouth, but when he saw Kristi's eyes watering, a tightness formed in his throat, so he decided not to press the subject. He stood and cleared his throat. "Let's go grab something to eat."

"I've been debating. I think it may be best if you go ahead without me," Kristi said.

Nash winced.

"My going to the police station doesn't sound like the best idea," Kristi continued, "since we're not sure who to trust, right?"

Nash agreed, but Kristi's tone insinuated a different reason for her not wanting to go.

"What about food? I know you're hungry."

"No, don't worry about that. There's something in the kitchen I can whip up."

"You sure?"

Kristi wiped the sniffles from her nose. "I'm sure," she said.

"Okay… I'll hafta borrow your car."

Kristi nodded. "Of course."

"Need anything before I go?"

She shook her head.

"Alright. I'll call you," Nash said before heading to the garage.

Nash took the Acura and grabbed a burger from a popular franchise. He found a parking spot and ate inside of the car. The patty was juicier and the bun more buttery than he remembered. He enjoyed it. He figured it was because it had been hours since he last ate, and he had worked up an appetite since. Just when he finished the burger, his phone rang.

"Detective Moore," he answered the phone between chews.

"Officer Nash. When can I expect you at the station?" Moore asked.

"I'll be heading that way soon. You heard we have a witness who can corroborate that I was framed?"

"From my understanding, the witness is a crooked cop. I'm not jumping to any conclusions until I get an official statement."

Nash ran his tongue across his teeth, wiping the leftover burger debris from them. "Jumping to conclusions," he said. "I know a thing or two about that."

Moore scoffed. "I'll see you soon."

The call ended.

Nash arrived at the police station twenty-three minutes later, entering through the same door he and Barnhill had exited the night before. He threaded through a group of uniformed officers on his way to the door next to the bullet-proof glass enclosure where the receptionist sat. To his surprise, his key fob worked. He thought Moore would've made sure all of his access was cut.

Guess not.

Nash stepped into a chattering bullpen crowded with offi-cers walking across the floor, escorting preps for processing, or sitting at their desks conversing with civilians. The aroma from both fresh and stale coffee circulated in the air in combination with the scent of unfinished takeout. It was a typical day at the station.

Nash spotted Moore standing near a hall on the west side of the building. The two men briefly locked eyes before Moore beckoned Nash with a wave. With his head on a swivel, Nash walked toward the detective.

"You made it," Moore said. He looked over Nash's shoulder. "Alone?"

Nash shrugged. "Why wouldn't I be?"

Moore grinned, his thick mustache rising as he did. "There's a reason I'm a detective."

"Which is?"

"I have an eye for sifting through information and getting to facts and truth."

Nash chuckled. "Facts and truth," he said. "Fact is, I was framed. Truth is, I should've never been arrested."

Moore sighed. "Let's talk more about that." He pivoted toward the hall. "Step into my office."

Nash followed Moore through the hallway and into a conference room. On the way inside, Nash noticed a uniformed officer wearing a cap near the end of the hall. The officer stood idle, pressing at his cellphone screen. Nash disregarded the scene and trailed Moore into the room.

Moore adjusted his blazer before sitting at a small circular table. "Have a seat," he offered.

Nash folded his arms and leaned against the wall next to the door. "I'll stand for now."

Moore shrugged and shook his head. "Whatever. Just make sure the door is closed."

"It is."

"Here's the deal. I haven't made it to the hospital yet to question Ward. And Fletcher just got back to his cell. He had some minor injuries when we found him at the aquarium." Moore's thick eyebrows furrowed.

Nash shrugged. "When can I talk to him?"

"Hold up. I'm working this case. You're not a detec—"

Nash pushed off the wall. "Don't give me that mess. I was framed. It's all connected. Frank Jackson's murder, the drugs and money, and these crooked behind cops. Don't hafta be a detective to see that."

"I know."

"You know what?"

"That you were framed."

Nash exhaled. He returned to the wall and folded his arms again.

"I had my doubts when I arrested you," Moore continued. "When I told Barnhill, he said I had to be mistaken. But I needed all the facts."

"And what are your facts so far?"

Moore looked at Nash. After a moment, he sighed, then stood. "All I'll say is that I agree with you."

Nash shrugged.

Moore exhaled again. "I believe it's all connected. As you know, the drugs and money were from a major bust involving a dangerous group of people."

"Yeah, a well-known Atlanta street gang."

"It goes higher than that."

"What? The mob?"

Moore nodded. "The Bianchi family, to be exact. The gang was just running for them."

"From what I've heard, that family has serious connections. So, that tracks with the moles inside the force."

"Yeah. I did an initial search for ties between the family and Fletcher and Ward. Nothing so far."

"What about Dent?"

Moore hunched his shoulders. "We just put a BOLO out on him less than an hour ago. Obviously, no hits yet."

"You're thinking the Bianchi family killed Frank Jackson?" Nash asked.

"That's my hunch. But I haven't been able to make a connection between Jackson and the family. Yet."

"Sounds like I know just as much as you do."

"I've only recently considered these angles, so maybe so."

Nash unfolded his arms as a thought occurred to him. "Do you know if Jackson and his wife were having issues?"

Moore winced at the question. "What kind of issues?"

"In their marriage."

"Why you ask?"

"Just making sure we're not missing something."

Moore contorted his lips. "No," he said, shaking his head. "They loved each other. At least that's what Mrs. Jackson told me."

"She told you that, but what do you think? What does your investigation say?"

"So far, I have no reason to believe they weren't happy. But you'd probably know more than me."

"What does that mean?"

"C'mon, Officer Nash. You don't think I know you've been spending time with his wife?"

Nash said nothing.

"I got the impression she didn't trust me very much," Moore continued. "Or any cop, for that matter. But she obviously trusts you. So what's the nature of your relationship with Mrs. Jackson?"

Nash glanced at the floor.

"Don't worry," Moore said. "I know you were investigating her husband's murder."

"How long have you known?"

"A few days now."

"Then why did you arrest me, man?"

"Procedure."

Nash scoffed and rolled his eyes.

Moore sighed, then he looked at Nash with a grave stare. "I believe there's a hit out on you. So, a part of me thought you'd be safe if you were held in jail and out of the way. I guess I was wrong."

"Yeah, I guess so. A hit, huh?"

"I thought I could get ahead of it, but I guess I was wrong about that, too. Talked with a few informants, including your guy Tony, and they all claimed they didn't know about a hit."

"How do you know about Tony?"

Moore chuckled. "Everyone uses Tony. When you become a detective, you'll understand."

"So you think I can be a detective?"

Moore cocked his head to the side and bounced a shoulder.

"I'll take that as a yes. Which is good, because I wanna speak to Fletcher."

TWELVE

Moore was initially hesitant but eventually agreed to Nash questioning Fletcher after Nash suggested, in no uncertain terms, that it was his investigating which exposed Fletcher and led to the crooked officer's arrest.

"You have five minutes," Moore informed Nash outside the interrogation room.

"That should be enough," Nash said.

Two uniformed officers walked past them and continued up the hall.

Moore pointed at a door eight feet away. "I'll be in the observation room, observing." He walked to the door, then aimed his palm at Nash with all five fingers stretched.

"Chill out, I got it," Nash said.

Moore entered the observation room. Nash watched until the door thumped closed behind the detective. Taking a deep breath, then exhaling, Nash entered the interrogation room. Perspiration peppered his arms under the apparent temperature hike, and a musty stench struck his nose. Nash wasn't surprised by either of the sensations. He knew the department had left the room in such a condition for a reason.

It made the suspect uncomfortable during the interrogation.

The room was rectangular, with a one-way mirror built into the north-facing wall. A square table sat at the center of the floor. There were two chairs at the table. One was empty. Fletcher sat in the other, facing the door. A glimmer from the overhead fluorescent reflected off his sweaty, cue ball head, and his beard covered his face like coarse nylon carpet. As Nash approached, he noticed a bandage on the back of Fletcher's head.

"That must hurt," Nash said while sliding the empty seat from the table.

Fletcher grimaced.

Nash sat. "Last time, you didn't answer my question," he said. "So I'll ask again. Other than you and Ward, who else is involved with this? And don't say Dent, I already know he's involved."

Fletcher looked down at the table and chuckled.

"Something funny?" Nash asked.

"You don't know what you're getting into," Fletcher said, slowly lifting his gaze to Nash's face.

Nash adjusted in his chair. "Okay. Help me understand what I'm getting into. Who are you working for?"

Fletcher pursed his lips, then folded his arms and leaned back in his chair.

"You don't want to talk?" Nash continued.

Fletcher said nothing.

"That's alright. The Bianchi family already believe you were the one who snitched their deal to the police."

"What deal?"

"The deal where their drugs and money were seized."

"I had nothing to do with that."

"That's not what they think."

Fletcher grinned. "You're terrible at bluffing," he said while looking at the wall to his right.

"Bluffing or not, you're a loose end. You know what they'll do to you if they even think you've turned on them."

Unfolding his arms, Fletcher adjusted in his chair, then glanced at Nash.

"Yeah. They got you scared," Nash said.

"I'd worry about myself if I was you. Sticking your nose in the wrong business can get you on… on a naughty list."

Nash's heart rate slightly increased. He breathed out slowly. "Naughty list," he said. "Oh, you mean a hit list."

Fletcher folded his arms again. "I didn't say that," he said before returning his attention to the wall.

"Don't worry about it. I know what you meant. But curious why I'm on that list. Was I getting too close to something?"

Fletcher shrugged. "I don't know what you're talking about."

Nash pushed away from the table, dragging his chair's legs across the epoxy concrete floor. "C'mon, Fletcher," he said while standing. "You just said I was on a hit list."

"I never said that."

"And you practically admitted to being involved in Frank Jackson's murder."

Fletcher whipped his head toward Nash. "Stop putting words in my mouth."

Nash leaned closer to the bald man. "Don'tcha think it's in your best interest to cooperate? I mean, the Bianchi family is coming after you either way."

Fletcher's eyebrows knitted.

"You're a loose end to them," Nash continued.

Fletcher's jaws tensed.

"And a rat."

Fletcher ejected from his seat, the chains around his ankles rattling as he did. "I ain't no rat," he said as he speared a finger toward Nash's face.

Nash yanked Fletcher's arm. He locked the bald man's shoulder before slamming him face first into the table.

Nash leaned toward Fletcher's ear. "Ya'll framed me, then tried to kill me," he said.

Fletcher grunted.

"My patience is wearing thin. I know you're on the Bianchi's payroll, and it's just a matter of time before we prove it."

Fletcher grunted again, lifting his head slightly off of the table.

Nash pushed him back down. "Where's Dent?"

"I don't know," Fletcher said, straining under the pressure of Nash's hold.

"Stop lying."

"I don't know! Last I heard from him was at the hotel."

"The Omni?"

"Yeah. Talked to him on the phone."

Nash loosened his grip as a thought occurred to him. A brisk knock vibrated from the one-way mirror.

Both Nash and Fletcher looked toward the mirror.

Another knock echoed, then another.

"Alright, alright, I'm lettin' him go," Nash said while completely releasing his hold on Fletcher.

The bald, bearded man fell back into his chair, panting.

Nash walked to the door before turning to Fletcher. "See you around," he said.

Fletcher scowled but said nothing.

Once in the hall, Nash removed the phone he had taken from Fletcher at the aquarium and navigated to the recent calls. As he did, he heard a door open but kept his attention on the phone.

With the most recent number highlighted, Nash pressed the OK button before holding the phone to his ear. When he looked up, he saw the same uniformed officer with the cap from earlier. The man had his back to Nash and faced the opposite end of the hall. The door to the observation room shut. Nash walked toward the door as the phone rang in his ear. On the third ring, he noticed the officer near the end of the hall stop. The man removed his phone and pressed at it. Ringing immediately stopped on Nash's side. The officer with the cap turned and looked at Nash.

"Hey!" Nash shouted.

The officer raced out of the hall. Nash stepped after the man but stopped when he heard groans flow from the observation room. Inside, Moore lay sprawled on the floor. As Nash approached Moore, he noticed a bloodstain the size of a half-dollar coin through the detective's shirt. Nash knelt over Moore and pulled the shirt up to inspect the detective's wound.

"Somebody get the paramedics!" Nash yelled toward the hall, his heart pounding in his chest.

He placed his index and middle finger to Moore's neck and sighed when he discovered both a pulse and the detective breathing. To his right, a box full of T-shirts with the words, *Police Department*, printed on them sat on the floor. Nash snagged a couple of shirts and pressed the pieces of clothing against Moore's side. The detective winced and moaned at the pressure.

"What happened?" came a voice from the hall.

Nash turned to see a slim, buzz-cut officer behind him. "Some uniform in a cap," Nash said. "Did you see him?"

The officer shook his head.

"Get over here. Keep pressure on the wound."

The slim officer rushed to take Nash's place while Nash headed for the door. He ran into a lady officer in the hall just outside of the observation room.

"What's going on?" she asked.

"Get the paramedics. Looks like a stab wound," Nash told her before hurrying out of the hall.

He raced in the direction he had last seen the officer in the cap. Figuring the man left the building, Nash dashed to the nearest exit and stepped outside into the parking lot. The sky darkened as the sun made its evening descent. Nash jogged through the lot, cars flanking him on either side as he searched for the man wearing the cap. Reaching the end of the parking lot with no sign of the man in sight, he wondered if he had lost the guy. He slowed his stride, but before he came to a complete stop, a figure zipped from behind a parked cargo van and toward the main street.

"Hey!" Nash shouted while chasing the man into the street.

Exhaust struck his nose, and headlamps momentarily blinded him as he danced around two honking cars and pursued the man across the street. The chase continued down a side road. Nash slowly closed the gap between them. He reached and snagged the man's cap. Messy, dirty-blond hair sprung from the man's head. Nash threw the cap onto the pavement and reached again. His fingertips were centimeters from the assailant's collar before the man made a sharp left turn into an alleyway. The trash containers from multiple establishments lined the sides of the alley. The man grabbed a box and tossed it, then knocked over a garbage bin.

Nash dodged the box but tripped over the bin. He growled as he stumbled to his feet and chased the man through a door. The temperature immediately dropped, and clanking kitchenware accompanied the aroma of various foods to overwhelm Nash's senses. The dirty-blond pushed through the kitchen staff on his way to a pair of stainless-steel swinging doors.

The doors opened into a dining area. Nash scanned the room. The floor had multiple dining tables, most filled with customers eating and chit-chatting. Near the front, the restaurant's host stood halfway out the front door, staring down the street. Nash threaded through the tables and to the front door.

He tugged the door completely open.

The host gasped.

"Police, excuse me," Nash said on his way outside.

The street was dark, but Nash saw a male figure running near an intersection. He raced after the man. When he turned the corner, the figure ducked into another alleyway. Nash removed his gun and pressed his back against the icy wall. He took in a deep breath, then exhaled before training his gun down the alley. The man wasn't in sight. Nash took two steps into the alleyway before bright lights flared from the corner of his eye and tires screeched behind him. He turned to find a dark cargo van erratically parked on the curb. Footsteps in the alley rapidly approached from behind him. Before Nash could turn, a hard object struck his skull, and his vision faded into blackness.

THIRTEEN

Through the blackness, a boisterous roar streamed from above. Nash opened his eyes to a squint. A blurry image came into view. He jolted his head to shake away the grogginess, but the stench from mechanical fluids wasn't helping his throbbing head. The blur in front of him moved, and a mumbling voice hit Nash's ears. He couldn't interpret the gibberish. It was muffled and low-pitched. Nash blinked and continued to jolt his head. The blurry figure slowly contoured into a man's face. Shortly after, the babble became more comprehensible.

"Nash," the man said. He raised a hand and snapped his middle finger and thumb. "Officer Derrick Nash."

Nash scoffed. "You," he said. "Look a lil different without your cap."

"Good, you're awake."

Nash attempted to move his arms but quickly discovered he was seated with his wrists duct-taped together behind his back.

"I need to know what you know."

Nash looked at the man but said nothing.

"Did you hear me? Why were you with Kristi Jackson? What do you know about her husband's murder?"

Nash looked away. He shook his head but said nothing.

The man glowered. He leaned closer to Nash, then delivered two quick slaps to his cheek. "Hey, hey. What do you know?"

"I know your name's Patrick Dent. I know you used to be a cop, but now you're just a lapdog for the Bianchis."

Dent stood straight at the waist. He sighed before turning and taking two steps toward a rusty, eroded sliding metal door.

While Dent had his back turned, Nash scanned the room for anything that was a clue to his whereabouts. Aluminum walls and ceiling. The worn epoxy concrete floor was helpful, but the biggest clue was the propeller motor in the corner behind him. On the wall to Nash's right, a table sat under a fogged plexiglass window. On top of the table rested Nash's cellphone, his gun, the flip phone he took from Fletcher, and the envelope he found in the safe at Kristi's house.

Dent turned just in time to catch Nash eyeing the table. He grinned before stepping to the table and removing Nash's gun. "So you know my name and who I work for."

"I guess I do now."

Dent chuckled. He wagged the gun at Nash as he approached the restrained man. "Good one," he said. "But you should know something. I'm the one who killed Jackson. I pulled the trigger."

The room went silent. A lump formed in Nash's throat. He gulped as he stared at Dent. Mainly because he believed the crooked ex-cop and was convinced he was more unhinged than Ward and Fletcher.

"And it doesn't matter," Dent continued while aiming the gun at Nash. "Because this isn't gonna end well for you, regardless. You've ruffled too many feathers."

Nash winced. "Whose feathers?"

"I'm asking the questions. Now tell me something, and maybe your life will be extended a few hours."

Nash's heart rate increased. His breathing increased too but was shallow. Thoughts raced through his head. He understood the danger of the situation but didn't think he'd actually die behind it. Especially at the hand of a crooked, used-to-be cop.

"Talk now," Dent said, his finger pulling back the trigger.

Nash steadied his breathing. "I don't know much."

"Then you're of no use," Dent continued, his finger slowly squeezing the trigger.

"Wait!" Nash protested.

FOURTEEN

Two hours earlier, Kristi sat on the couch in her living room, enjoying a tuna salad sandwich she had prepared just moments after Nash left. For condiments, she added lettuce, tomatoes, some pickles, mayo, mustard, and a few tears. She had a moment while making the sandwich. She'd been having such moments since Frank died. A few tears here, a few tears there, never turning the faucet completely open. She often felt she was suppressing her hurt but would brush it off, convincing herself she was too busy to grieve.

She took her plate to the kitchen after finishing her sandwich. Leaning across the kitchen island on her elbow, she scrolled through her phone. No missed calls. No messages. She stood straight, and her eyebrows knitted as a thought came to her. Leaving the kitchen, she made a beeline for Frank's office. The overhead lamp briefly hummed before pouring white LED light across the room. Kristi hurried to the desk and searched the drawers. Unsurprisingly, she didn't find anything she didn't expect.

"What did you find, Derrick?" she grumbled while scanning the room.

Her eyes stopped at the picture hanging in front of the safe.

She hurried to the artwork and removed it from the wall, exposing the safe. After entering the safe's code, she rummaged inside. Not finding anything new, she sighed and shook her head. "I don't know what I expected."

She went to close the safe but noticed something she hadn't before. A slit at the bottom of the safe. Kristi slid her fingers around the area and discovered a compartment door. She opened the door, but the compartment was empty. Kristi contorted her lips, and her eyebrows furrowed as her mind wandered about the various possibilities. After a few moments in that state, she replaced everything and returned to the living room. She plopped onto the couch and tilted her head on the sofa's back cushion. Her eyes closed.

An hour later, they opened wide to a loud buzz. It took her a moment to realize the buzzing came from outside at the front gate. Kristi sprang from the couch, nearly tripping over a fallen throw pillow on her way to the front door. A small monitor near the door displayed a dark-colored sports car parked at the gate.

Kristi pressed the intercom button below the monitor. "Who is this?" she asked into the microphone next to the button.

On the monitor, a woman with straight, dark hair craned from the car's driver-side window toward the gate's panel. She pressed at the panel, then spoke.

"Kristi Jackson?" the woman's soft voice came through the monitor's speakers. She had a slight Italian accent.

"Yes. Who are you?"

"We need to talk."

"Do you live here?"

"No."

"How'd you get past security?"

"I know Joseph."

Kristi winced.

"Can I come in?"

"Not until I know who you are?"

"I… I knew your husband."

"What? How?"

The woman swiveled her head. She glanced at the back of her car, toward the street. "It's best we talk in person," she said, returning her attention to the intercom.

Kristi briefly pulled away from the intercom. She squinted and bit her top lip before leaning back toward the microphone. "Are you alone?"

"Yes," the woman said, shrugging while pointing to the inside of her car. "It's important. Are you working with a cop —Nash—Derrick Nash?"

"What's wrong? Is he okay?"

The woman swiveled her head again, and from the monitor, Kristi could tell she breathed out a heavy sigh.

"I'm not sure," the woman admitted through the intercom.

Kristi drummed her fingers against the wall. "Hold on," she told the woman before removing her cellphone.

She dialed Nash's number, but it went straight to voicemail. Patting the cellphone against her empty palm, Kristi considered what she should do next.

"Are you there?" the woman asked through the speaker.

"Come to the front," Kristi said while pressing a slightly larger button next to the intercom button.

The gate unlocked, then slid open. As the woman drove through, Kristi rushed to a closet in the living room. She pushed the hanging clothing to the side and knelt at the rear of the closet. After shuffling a couple of boxes around, she found a small black case. There were two more cases just like it in different areas of the house.

Kristi remembered when Frank first brought the cases home. He was beside himself. A little frantic but had quickly calmed when he saw Kristi worrying. Initially, she didn't understand why they needed what was in the cases, but over the past couple of weeks, it had become more apparent why.

Inside the case lay a black pistol and magazine. Kristi inserted the magazine into the pistol, just like Frank had showed her, then returned to the front door. She peeped through the window and saw white LED headlights approaching the house. The dark blue Porsche swung into the driveway. Its engine revved as the vehicle parked parallel to the front of the house. The car's passenger-side windows were slightly tinted, but Kristi saw the silhouettes of the car seats and the woman behind the wheel. The Porsche's engine purred to a stop. Shortly after, the woman exited the car.

Kristi opened the front door and stepped outside. The woman from the car circled to the passenger side but paused when she noticed Kristi standing at the door with a gun in hand. The woman's honey-toned skin and red lipstick glimmered under the door lamp's glow. She looked at Kristi through brown, almond-shaped eyes.

The woman chuckled as she brushed a hand through her straight black hair. "You don't need that," she said.

"We'll see about that, won't we?" Kristi quickly replied, craning her neck toward the car and glancing the vehicle over. "Are you alone?"

The woman nodded. "Yes."

"Is Derrick okay?"

The woman shook her head. "I'm not sure," she answered with a shrug. "Can we talk inside?"

"Who are you? How do you know my husband?"

The woman glanced at the ground. "We—um—we worked together."

"He never mentioned you."

"We didn't work together for very long. But he never mentioned he was married either." The woman sighed. "May I please come in?"

Kristi nodded, then side-stepped as the woman passed through the door.

"Okay, we have to—" the woman started.

Kristi closed the door. "Who are you?" she asked while clenching the pistol at her side.

"Take it easy."

"I asked a question."

The woman released a nervous chuckle. "My name is Francesca, Francesca Bianchi."

FIFTEEN

"Why does that name sound familiar?" Kristi asked.

"My family does have quite the reputation," Francesca said.

"Are they famous?"

Francesca half smiled. "You can say that," she said.

Kristi's eyebrows knitted. "Wait. Bianchi. The crime family?"

Francesca nodded. "Yeah, but not all of us are bad."

"Why would my husband be working with you?"

Francesca glanced at the gun in Kristi's hand.

Kristi looked at the pistol before stuffing it into her front waistband. "I won't shoot you, for now at least."

"Are you sure you want to hear this?"

"Pretty sure."

"He was laundering money for my family."

"Really?" Kristi said while looking Francesca up and down. "You're not all bad, huh?"

"I had nothing to do with that."

"You just said you were working with Frank. And he was laundering money for your family, so it certainly sounds like you had something to do with it."

"I didn't know."

"Right."

"I'm only here to help."

"Help? How?"

"I think your cop friend may be in trouble."

Kristi jolted her head. She got caught up with Frank's involvement and almost forgot about Nash. "Yeah—where—is he okay?"

Francesca shrugged a shoulder. "I'm not sure. I overheard one of my father's guys talking on the phone. He mentioned they caught him and was holding him."

Kristi's eyes widened. "What? Why didn't you mention this before?" She dug into her pocket and removed her cell phone. "We have to call the cops."

Francesca gestured for Kristi to stop. "No. My family is connected. Can't be sure who to trust."

"Then what are we supposed to do?"

"I think I know where they took him."

Kristi stood in her thoughts for a moment. She wasn't sure if she could trust this Francesca woman, but she didn't see another option. "Take me there," she said.

Francesca winced. "Are you sure?"

"You said you came to help. Prove it. Take me there."

"Okay. It's just, it could be dangerous."

Kristi patted the pistol in her waistband. "I'm taking this with me," she said.

The two women entered the Porsche. Kristi eased in through the passenger side while Francesca slid in behind the wheel.

Francesca put the car into gear, then sped out of the drive-way. Kristi jerked back into the seat. She gaped at Francesca, then frowned.

"I'm sorry," Francesca said with a slight grin.

Kristi was about to say something but didn't because she

figured it was probably a good thing Francesca drove fast if Derrick was in trouble.

Francesca maintained a brisk speed until they reached the security hut. She slowed, then jerked to a stop. Joseph exited the hut with a smile on his face.

"Ms. Francesca," he said while approaching the car.

His smile morphed into a frown when he noticed Kristi sitting in the passenger seat.

"Oh, hi, Mrs. Jackson."

Kristi rolled her eyes. "We're a bit rushed."

"Sure," Joseph said on his way back inside the hut.

The gate's arms lifted, and Francesca sped through, then veered onto the main road.

"Seems like Joseph knows you very well," Kristi said.

Francesca glanced at her but said nothing.

They drove mostly in silence for another twenty minutes before Francesca made a left turn down a dark dirt road. The Porsche rocked and bounced along the path until its tires hit pavement and smoothed the ride. The car approached a tall chain-link fence that had obviously seen better days. Parts of the chain mesh were missing, and many of the fence posts were bent or leaning.

"Where are we?" Kristi asked.

Just as she uttered the last syllable in her inquiry, a plane roared overhead.

"Wait, this is the old hangar yard near the airport."

Francesca nodded.

"Are you sure Derrick is here?"

"I'm sure," Francesca said. "Sometimes I overhear my father's men talking. It's amazing the things you learn in a house when the men think you're just an unassuming, cute pair of legs."

Kristi glanced at her. She understood what Francesca meant but wasn't sure why the obviously troubled woman was helping. Kristi had a hunch but hoped it wasn't the reason.

Francesca crept the Porsche toward a group of small, worn aluminum hangars. She parked near a plot of grass, a spot not easily visible from the hangars' doors. Switching off the head-lights, she fixed on a dark cargo van parked near the hangar.

Kristi noticed. "You've seen that van before?" she asked.

Francesca nodded. "I think so. At my father's house. It belongs to one of his guys."

"That means you could be right. Derrick is here."

Francesca looked at Kristi. "Yeah," she said with a sigh.

"What's wrong?"

Francesca glanced past the parked van and at the hangar. She shook her head. "Nothing. Just…"

Kristi leaned toward her with knitted eyebrows. "Just what?"

Francesca scoffed. "The guy who drives the van some-times does clean up with a cop that works for my father."

"Clean up?"

"The cop's kinda crazy, too."

"Clean up?" Kristi repeated.

Francesca stared at her. "Yeah," she said, nodding gravely.

A knot formed in Kristi's gut as she looked at the hangar. "Before we do anything, I need to make a call," she said.

SIXTEEN

Inside the hangar, the door slid open, and a tall, wiry man with his hair fixed in a man bun entered the room. He wore all black, like a cat burglar. Like he had unsavory plans and dressed to blend with the shadows to conceal his activities.

"Hey—" the man started, his pointy nose crinkled. "Whatchu doing?"

"What I'm paid to do," Dent told him. "What is it?"

"We've got company."

Dent dropped the pistol to his side. "Saved by the bell," he told Nash.

Nash sat glaring at Dent. He panted but said nothing.

Dent chuckled. "Don't worry. I'm not gonna kill you, at least not yet. My boss wants to speak to you first. He's here now."

"It's not the boss," the all-black-wearing, pointy nose man said.

Dent whipped his head in the man's direction. "Who is it then?"

The man nodded toward the door. "Come see for yourself," he said on his way out of the room.

Dent sighed. He rolled his eyes, then fixed on Nash. "I'll be back. Don't go anywhere now."

Nash watched as Dent left the room. When the door shut behind the crooked ex-cop, Nash jerked in his chair and tugged against the duct tape restraining his hands. He peered around the room, hoping to find something that could help free him. He found nothing. And the tape was unyielding.

"Great," Nash growled, smacking his back against the chair's backrest. "Not good."

Faint voices flowed from the opposite side of the door.

"Why are you here?" Dent said.

A softer voice said something, then there was a bout of silence.

"What are you doing?"

"Wait, hey."

Thumping and racket followed. A moment later, footsteps approached the door. Nash watched through squinted eyes as the door eased open. Dent entered with a grim expression on his face. As he continued into the room, a pistol aimed at his back followed. Holding the pistol was a familiar woman. It took Nash a minute to place her. The woman in the photo. The same photo inside of the envelope on top of the table only feet away from him.

She nodded at Nash, her shiny black hair bouncing as she did. "Untie him," she told Dent in an Italian accent.

Dent smirked.

"Now!" the woman jabbed the gun at him.

Dent walked toward Nash. "This isn't smart, little lady," he said. "I don't think your father will approve."

"You let me worry about my father. Just do as I say."

Dent stepped behind Nash and reached into his own pocket. The woman jabbed the gun at him again. The ex-cop slowly raised his hand and produced a pocket knife.

"Don't get cute," the woman said. "I will shoot you."

Dent squatted, and Nash felt pressure against his wrists,

followed by a scratching as the used-to-be cop sawed at the tape. The tape gave and Nash yanked his hands apart, then stood. An acid, vinegary scent struck his nose as he lifted his arms to eye level and removed the remaining tape from his wrists. Nash quickly turned to Dent. He eyed the dirty ex-cop hard. Dent grinned. Nash took the pocketknife away from him.

"Now what, tough guy?" Dent taunted.

Nash dropped the knife at Dent's feet. As the ex-cop's eyes followed the blade, Nash delivered a devastating right cross to his jaw. Dent leaned to the side. His eyes closed, and he dropped to the floor, knocked out cold. Nash hurried to the table and grabbed his belongings. After placing them inside his pockets, he glanced at the woman. She had lowered the gun and stood staring at him.

"Who are you?" he asked her.

She winced. "Those are the first words you say? How about, thank you?"

"Thank you? Your people caused all of this. I heard him say your father. You're a Bianchi."

"I'm not part of my family's dealings. And my name is Francesca."

"What are you a part of, then?" Nash asked as he ejected the magazine from his gun and inspected it before reinserting it back into the pistol. "Breaking up other families?"

"You realize I just saved you?"

"Yeah. Just wondering why. Excuse me," Nash said while training his gun at the door.

He eased the door open and peeked through the slit. On the hangar's main floor, Kristi stood holding a gun. Nash wasted no time in opening the door completely and stepping onto the main floor. Kristi had her gun aimed at the pointy nose guy with the man bun. Her eyes lit up when she saw Nash.

"You're okay," she said.

"Yeah. But why are you here?"

"What do you mean?"

Francesca came up behind Nash. "We should leave," she said, making her way toward the hangar's sliding door.

Nash jabbed his thumb in Francesca's direction. "You came with her?" he asked Kristi.

She shrugged. "You were in trouble."

"We should leave," Francesca repeated. "Now."

"Okay," Kristi said. She then nodded at the pointy nose man in the suit. "But what should we do with him?"

"Tie him up or knock him out," Francesca said.

"Why you in such a rush?" Nash asked Francesca.

Pointy nose chuckled. "She's probably tryna get out of town before her father finds out what she's done."

"He's your father; he's not going to kill you," Kristi said.

The pointy nose man scoffed. "You obviously don't know Ray Bianchi," he said.

"Shut up," Nash told him. "We're not leaving. We gonna call the cops. And while they're on the way, you gonna answer my questions."

As Nash finished uttering the last sentence, an engine hummed outside the hangar. Headlights briefly glared through the hangar window, and the vehicle's brakes squeaked.

Kristi glanced at the side door before looking at Nash. "Who's that?" she asked no one in particular.

"You're expecting your boss?" Nash asked the tall, pointy nose man.

The man didn't answer. He just smirked.

Francesca raced to the window. "I can't see anything," she said before rushing to the door. She opened it, then peeped outside. "It's my dad," she said, ducking back inside.

"You sure?" Kristi asked her.

"Yes. I can spot his Suburban anywhere."

"Was he by himself?" Nash asked Francesca on his way to the door.

Before she could answer, he opened the door and took a peek. He saw a lean man in a formal suit exit the Suburban's front passenger side door with a submachine gun in hand.

The man with the submachine gun walked to the back door and opened it. Another man with good posture stepped out. Surveying the area, he unbuttoned his blazer. A stubbier fellow in a suit exited from behind the wheel, then circled to the back of the vehicle and opened the trunk. He removed a submachine gun similar to the other guy's before shutting the trunk and joining the other two men on the passenger side.

"What's happening?" Kristi asked.

Nash held up a finger, requesting silence.

The three men outside stood in somewhat of a huddle, conversing. A moment after, the one with good posture removed a pistol and pointed in Nash's direction. Nash quickly ducked back inside and locked the door.

"Ready to share?" Kristi asked him.

"Yeah, really." Francesca followed up.

"There's three of 'em. Armed. Machine guns."

"Machine guns?" Kristi repeated.

"Would you say your father has good posture?" Nash asked Francesca.

Her eyebrows furrowed. "I guess so—actually, yes, he does," she answered with a shrug.

The pointy nose man chuckled. "You're all dead," he said to the group before focusing on Francesca. "Even you, princess."

Francesca stepped to him. "Shut up!" She aimed her gun at him, then wagged the pistol toward the sliding door near the front of the hangar. "Go."

The man turned. Francesca gripped her gun's barrel, cocked her arm back and, reaching high, struck the back of the man's head. She let out a loud cry that suggested she had given it all she had. And it showed because the pointy nose man immediately sunk to the floor and fell to his side.

"Why did you do that?" Kristi asked.

Francesca shrugged. "We don't have time to tie him up."

Kristi looked at Nash.

"He'll be out for a while. One less person to deal with," he told her.

"Okay, but what do we do now?" Kristi asked.

"My car's out there," Francesca said. "I'm sure my father saw it. I'll make a scene and talk with him. Try to lead them to the front while you two escape out the side door."

"Risky," Nash said. "Won't take him long to figure out what you did."

"Yeah, sounds dangerous, Francesca," Kristi said.

"Do you have a better idea?" Francesca asked.

Nash and Kristi said nothing.

"Okay. We'll go with my plan."

The side door's knob turned.

Francesca stuffed her gun into her back waistband. "I must be pazzo," she said before jogging to the sliding door.

The side door's knob rattled. Nash and Kristi pressed against the wall. The rattling intensified. Nash glanced in Francesca's direction and saw she had made it to the front sliding door. Thumps flowed from the side door.

Nash looked at Kristi and moved his finger to his mouth.

She nodded.

The sliding door scraped open. The thumps from the side door strengthened. Nash expected gunfire to soon follow. But in the brief silence between thumps, when he expected gunshots, Francesca screamed. Nash glanced and saw her hanging out the sliding door, frantically yelling in Italian. The activity at the side door stopped, and on the opposite side, footsteps raced along the length of the hangar toward the front.

Nash nodded at Kristi, then unlocked the door. He poked

his head outside and saw the stubby man rounding the hangar's front corner. The moment the man disappeared around the corner, Nash fully opened the door and grabbed Kristi's hand.

"Let's go," he said, pulling her along as he rushed outside.

They made it two yards from the hangar before a loud, familiar voice yelled after them.

"They're over here!"

SEVENTEEN

Nash glanced over his shoulder and saw Dent leaning against the doorjamb. The ex-cop pointed and hollered after Nash and Kristi. Automatic gunfire roared over Dent's shouting. Nash grabbed Kristi's arm and pulled her along as they took cover behind the cargo van.

"Get down!" he yelled while covering Kristi with his body as her screams drowned under the gunfire.

Bullets ripped through the van's frame and windows, ricocheting off metal and shattering glass. When the thunderous booms ceased, Nash erected with his gun extended across the van's hood, aimed at the hangar's side door. The stocky man in the suit stood at the door, fighting to insert a fresh magazine into his machine gun. He was successful, but as he brought his gun to bear, Nash fired three rounds. The shots clapped and tore across the sky. All three bullets hit the stubby suit, center mass. The man dropped his gun and stumbled backward into the darkness of the hangar.

The pistol emitted a sulfurous stench, which Nash inhaled while quickly ducking back behind the van. Kristi sat curled with her arms over her head and her gun shaking in her hand. Retreat was the best option in Nash's mind, especially considering her lack of experience with gunfights.

He reached for her hand. "Let's go."

She shook her head.

"We gotta go," Nash said before glancing over the van's hood and at the hangar's side door. "They're gonna be on us soon."

She grabbed his hand, and Nash pulled her off the ground. They ran toward a neighboring hangar. Shouts and more gunfire followed them. The rumble from a plane streaming above obscured the shouts and gunfire as Nash and Kristi entered through the shabby hangar's rust stricken half-missing door. Bullets punctured what remained of the door. The gun's blasts intensified as the bird in the sky crossed above. Nash and Kristi raced toward the back of the structure.

They danced around a small, tattered aircraft frame, engine parts, and crates. Nash caught a whiff of fuel as they scurried behind a large canister. Footsteps rapidly approached the door. Nash peeked around the container and saw a lean silhouette enter the hangar.

"Is this a petrol tank?" Kristi whispered, her nose crinkled.

Nash nodded. "We need to move," he whispered back.

The dark figure threaded through the hangar's various equipment and storage containers. The man had his submachine gun aimed as he slowly approached the back.

With his index finger to his lips, Nash turned to Kristi. He pointed at a dilapidated office to their right. It wasn't the most ideal place to retreat, but despite its broken windows and battered door, it was their best option. They tiptoed toward the space while sirens faintly echoed in the distance. Kristi didn't seem too bothered by it. They crept into the office and took cover behind a worn but sturdy metal desk that had been flipped on its side.

"Stay here," Nash told Kristi.

She shook her head while grabbing his arm. "Wait—where are you going?"

"We can't both stay here. Need to go on the offensive."

"Are you trying to protect me? Just stay put, and we'll wait it out."

Nash gently removed her hand from his arm. "You're gonna hafta trust me," he said. "If anyone besides me comes through this door, you shoot 'em."

In a crouch, he crept to the office door.

"Wait," Kristi called to him, doing her best to maintain a whisper.

He turned to her and placed his index finger on his lips.

She shook her head, and her body relaxed into a sigh.

Footsteps skulked toward them. Kristi ducked behind the desk while Nash exited the office. He hid behind a crate, then peeked around its corner. A submachine gun's barrel came into view on the opposite side of the fuel canister. The lean man in the suit followed.

Nash aimed his gun at the man but lowered it when the suit stopped near the canister. Nash didn't want to hit the canister by mistake. It could create a very bad day for everyone close by. The machine-gun-toting man pivoted in Nash's direction. Nash dodged behind the crate. As the man's footsteps approached, Nash inched around to the opposite side of the crate and waited. He felt the man's presence. A tingling sensation pulsed through his body and made the hairs on his arms rise. The footsteps stopped, and the man's breathing intensified. A moment later, the footsteps continued, but away from the crate. Nash was relieved until he realized the man was heading toward the office. Kristi crossed his mind, and he immediately sprang into action.

The man spun as Nash rushed him. Before the suit could bring his gun to bear, the beat cop was on him. Nash controlled his opponent's gun with his free hand while delivering an elbow to the lean man's throat with the arm that held his own pistol. It was a technique he had learned at the academy. The man's machine gun dropped to the pavement. He reached for his throat as he stumbled backwards and smacked back first into a wall. Nash lifted his pistol, but before he could raise the gun to chest height, the lean man bounced from the wall and tackled him. The two men, along with Nash's pistol, fell to the floor.

Straddling Nash, the lean man threw a jab at his face. Nash weaved his head out of the punch's trajectory. The man's knuckles cracked against the concrete floor. He yelped while drawing his hand back toward his chest and caressing it. Nash quickly grabbed a fistful of the man's shirt, then caught his chin with a punch. The suit rolled off Nash and onto his knees. Nash hustled to his feet and delivered a devastating kick to his opponent's rib cage. The man groaned before rolling onto his back, coughing. Nash straddled him, then rocked his jaw with a solid right cross. The man's head bounced off the pavement. He was knocked out cold.

Kristi raced from the office. "You okay?" she asked.

Nash stood and nodded. A boom stuffed the air, and the sound of metal ricocheting off metal rang behind him just feet away from his ear.

"I missed," a familiar voice shouted.

Nash peered through the darkness and saw Dent's silhouette rapidly approaching with a limp.

"Careful, you idiot. That's a gas canister," a separate, agitated but confident voice said.

Nash nudged Kristi toward a large wooden container. "Go!" he said before darting to a dark corner and kneeling. He watched as Kristi squatted behind the container. Dent's footsteps approached fast with a ginger rhythm. When he rounded the gas canister, Nash sprung from the corner, gripping the used-to-be-cop's gun-carrying hand and his throat. Dent's back smacked into the wall perpendicular to the office. Nash shoved Dent's gun-holding hand into the wall. Dent grunted under the pain. Nash increased the pressure around his opponent's neck and rammed his hand against the wall again. Dent dropped the gun but quickly kneed Nash's inner thigh. Nash jerked forward, inadvertently loosening his hold on Dent's hand and throat.

The corrupt ex-cop broke free and shoved Nash before throwing a wild cross at him. Nash parried the punch, but the force sent him stumbling backward. As Nash struggled to find his footing, he noticed three things unfolding seemingly in slow motion. First, the man with good posture, Ray Bianchi, came into view near the gas canister, grappling with a fighting Francesca. Second, Kristi raced from behind the crate. The third and final thing, which quickly became the priority, was Dent arching toward his gun on the floor.

Nash rushed toward him. Heaving his pistol from the floor, Dent pivoted to Nash. While the used-to-be cop fought to bring his gun to bear, Nash jostled him, but not before he got a shot off. The bullet penetrated the floor, and the gun flung from Dent's hand. The two men slammed into the wall again. Dent caught Nash in the stomach with a jab. Nash retaliated with a cross to the corrupt ex-cop's face.

Dent staggered a few steps before grimacing and producing a blade. "This is the same knife I used to stab your buddy, Moore," he said.

"He ain't my buddy," Nash said.

"Kill him already," Bianchi said while trying to maintain control of Francesca.

With the knife pointed at Nash, Dent stepped toward him.

Nash shuffled backward, and as Dent pursued him, a loud boom echoed through the hangar, drowning out the approaching sirens.

Dent stopped dead in his tracks. A circle of blood formed on his chest as he dropped the knife and sank to the pavement.

Nash turned and found Kristi holding Dent's fallen pistol.

Smoke steamed from the barrel as he walked to her. She kept the gun aimed in Dent's direction. The pistol bouncing in her hands as her body trembled.

"It's okay," Nash said, placing his hand on the gun.

Before he could grab the pistol from her, a scream and groan clamored over the wailing sirens.

Francesca had bitten Bianchi, and in return, he slapped her. She fell and sprawled on the floor.

Bianchi trained his pistol on Nash. "Don't even think about it," he said. "Drop the gun."

Nash nodded at Kristi, and she allowed the pistol to fall to the floor without hesitation.

Nash shook his head. "What are you doing?" he said to Bianchi. "It's over. You can hear they're on the way."

Bianchi smirked. "You think I'm worried about the cops?" he said with a slight chuckle. "I know enough people for that not to concern me much."

Nash inhaled a shaky breath.

"Why did you kill Frank?" Kristi asked.

"It was business," Bianchi continued. "He got too smart for his own good. Attempted to take down my organization from within."

"I don't understand why Frank would work for someone like you."

Bianchi winced. "Oh, you don't know?"

Nash shook his head slightly and sighed.

Bianchi looked at Francesca as she sat on the floor. "You mean my treacherous daughter didn't tell you she was—"

"She didn't have to," Kristi interrupted. "I figured it out, just needed to confirm. You used their affair to blackmail him into working for you."

"What now?" Nash said. "You're gonna kill the two of us and get off?"

"Three," Bianchi said, looking in Francesca's direction. "As much as it pains—" His eyes widened.

Francesca had the pistol Nash dropped aimed at Bianchi.

"You're going to shoot your father?" he said, his face oozing confusion.

"Just give up and turn yourself in," Francesca said, the pistol quaking in her hands.

The confused look on Bianchi's face morphed into anger. He swung his aim toward Francesca. "You ingrato little—"

Two blasts roared. Out of pure instinct, Nash covered Kristi. He sank to the ground with her in his arms and snatched Dent's pistol, the gun Kristi dropped just moments before, from the floor. Nash turned with the gun aimed in Bianchi's direction. Bianchi doubled over and hugged his stomach. Francesca sat on the floor with her gun trained on him. She watched with wide eyes and quivering lips as her father dropped to his knees, then fell face down on the pavement.

EIGHTEEN

Siren echoes surrounded the hangar. Flashing red and blue lights shone through the windows and seeped through the holes and gaps in the hangar's structure. Nash nudged Kristi to arm's length.

"You alright?" he asked her.

She nodded before turning to Francesca. Nash looked in the same direction and saw Francesca sitting in the same spot with the gun pointed at where her father had stood just moments before.

"Stay here," he told Kristi.

She nodded again.

Nash walked to Francesca and squatted next to the panting woman.

"It's okay," he told her while slowly drawing the gun from her hands. "I'll take this."

She stared into space with her mouth slightly gaped as Nash helped her to her feet. She was clearly in shock.

"You okay?" Nash asked her.

She didn't answer.

"Francesca?"

"Huh?" she said.

Nash saw confusion cloud her exotic almond-shaped brown eyes. "You okay?" he asked.

"Ah, yeah."

Nash looked at Kristi. "Okay. Let's get up outta here."

The group walked toward the front of the hangar. When they were ten feet away from the hangar's half-missing, bullet-hole-filled door, police officers rushed inside and flooded the area, shouting demands with their guns drawn.

Nash quickly raised his arms. "I'm a cop!" he said.

Kristi and Francesca raised their arms as the officers continued barking demands.

"I'm a cop!" Nash repeated.

"Wait! Stand down!" a familiar voice commanded. Chris threaded through a group of officers on his way into the hangar. "He's one of us."

The officers lowered their guns. Nash did the same with his arms. Kristi and Francesca followed suit.

"How'd you know where we were?" Nash asked Chris.

"You left me a message," Chris said.

Nash squinted and cocked his head to the side. "No, I didn't."

"Who else calls me Big C? Big C, your friend needs your help at this address. That's the message I got."

"Wasn't me."

"It was me," Kristi said.

Nash turned to her.

"What?" she said while shrugging. "I listen to you."

Nash smiled.

"Anybody else in here?" Chris asked.

"Three bodies," Nash said. "All perps. One is Ray Bianchi."

Chris winced. "Fo' real?"

Nash bounced a shoulder.

Chris shook his head and sighed. "Let's get you guys outta here."

As the group crowded outside, Chris shared his gaze between Nash, Kristi, and Francesca.

"We're gonna need a statement from all of you."

"Of course," Nash said.

Kristi and Francesca both nodded soberly. Two paramedics approached the group. A man and a woman.

"We need to check you out," the woman said.

Chris placed his hand on Nash's shoulder. "I need to holla at you for a second."

As the two men stepped away, the paramedics led Kristi and Francesca toward the ambulance. Kristi looked back at Nash and forced a smile. He did the same.

"What's up?" Nash asked Chris.

"I need to know what happened, man. From you. We'll get a full statement later, but I heard you were at the police station, then Moore—"

"How is he?"

"He's in the hospital, but stable."

"It was Dent. He snuck into the station, attacked Morris, then ambushed me outside. That's how I ended up here. He also killed Frank Jackson at Ray Bianchi's order."

"Why?"

"Frank Jackson was an accountant. They blackmailed him into laundering money for them. But Frank had other plans, so Bianchi had him killed."

"Plans?"

Nash shrugged. "He probably tried to expose their operation or low-key report them to the authorities."

Chris nodded. "Hm. I wonder how they got him to play along to begin with."

"He was sleeping with Ray Bianchi's daughter."

Chris's eyes widened, and his mouth gaped. "What? That's crazy. Frank Jackson's wife is beautiful. Bianchi's daughter must be bad."

Nash looked at Francesca, who was being checked by the

female paramedic. "She's a good-looking woman," he said before looking at Kristi standing near the back of the ambulance. "But like you said, he already had a beautiful woman he was supposed to be committed to. Stupid move on his part."

Nash walked toward Kristi.

"So the woman with the long black hair is Bianchi's daughter?" Chris said to Nash's back. "I don't know, Derrick. Can we call the man stupid?"

Nash threw a dismissal wave at Chris as he made his way over to Kristi. The male paramedic finished attaching a bandage to her shoulder when Nash approached the ambulance.

"Everything else looks fine," the paramedic said.

"Thanks," Kristi said.

The man circled to the front of the vehicle, and Kristi pivoted to Nash.

"Just a scratch," she said, rubbing the bandage on her shoulder.

Nash stepped next to her and leaned against the ambulance. "Thank you," he said.

Kristi's eyebrows furrowed. "For what?"

"Saving my life."

"Well, you saved me first, didn't you?"

The two smiled, then stared at each other.

Their moment was interrupted as something caught Kristi's eye.

"I wonder how she's doing?" she said.

Nash looked past a crowd of busy officers and saw Francesca wrapped in a blanket, using a bucket for a seat.

"Really?" Nash said.

Kristi sighed. "Yeah, believe it or not."

They walked over, and Francesca looked up as they approached.

"How are you?" Nash asked her.

"I'm okay," she said in a somber tone. "Just a few bruises." She looked at Kristi. "I'm sorry. I didn't—"

"Let's not worry about that right now," Kristi said.

"You think I'm going to prison?" Francesca asked Nash.

Nash pursed his lips, shook his head, and hunched his shoulders all in one motion. "I don't know."

Francesca dropped her head.

"But I'm gonna make sure they know what you did here today."

She looked up and forced a smile. Both Nash and Kristi returned the gesture.

Two hours later, they were all at the police station. Nash had just finished explaining everything to the detective filling in for Moore before entering the detainment waiting room.

Francesca sat in the room alone, the blanket still covering her.

"The detective wanna talk with you," Nash told her. "He'll be out in a minute to get you."

She nodded but said nothing.

"After explaining everything to him, I think you'll be alright. It'll be bumpy, but I think you'll manage."

Francesca again nodded without speaking.

"Okay. Well, I'm gonna—"

"You know I loved him," she said.

Nash wasn't sure who she meant specifically, so he said nothing.

"Then he was taken from me," she continued. "I mean, I know now he was married, but... I miss him. And how my father took advantage of our relationship."

"It's pretty messed up all around. Imagine what the woman who married him is going through."

"Yeah, I know."

Nash looked around the room. "Speaking of which, where is Kristi?"

"She said she was going to the vending machine."

Nash turned to the table at the center of the room. Two wrapped sandwiches sat on top.

"We have sandwiches," he said.

Francesca shrugged. "Maybe she wanted chips with it," she said, "or after the day we had, chocolate."

The door Nash had entered through moments before swung open, and a lean man with dark, messy hair stepped halfway inside the room.

"Ms. Bianchi?" he said.

Both Nash and Francesca looked at him, then at each other.

"That's him," Nash told her.

Francesca sighed, then stood. She took three steps toward the door before stopping and turning to face Nash.

"You're a good cop and seem like a good man," she said. "Don't lose that."

She brushed past the detective as they both exited the room. Nash stood and watched the door shut. He drew in a deep breath, then exhaled before leaving the room himself. Fifteen seconds later, he approached the vending machines in the hall.

"Stupid machine," he heard Kristi's voice as he rounded the corner. She nudged the snack machine. "Just took my money. Why do they use these old machines?" She threw her arms up in a surrender posture.

"Sometimes you have to shake it," Nash said, stepping around her and grabbing the vending dispenser like he was giving it a hug.

He rocked the machine from side to side. A candy bar flipped over a spiral ring, then fell. Nash squatted and reached inside the dispenser door. As he stood with the candy bar in hand, Kristi stared at it.

She closed her eyes. "I wanted the pretzels," she said, her voice cracking.

"Okay, we can do that," Nash said while turning back to the vending machine.

As Nash reached for his wallet, he heard a deep gasp followed by weeping. Kristi palmed her face and cried. It confused Nash, but not really. He never saw her cry during the entire time he had known her. Like she felt she had to be strong. That can only go on for so long before it breaks a person.

Nash stepped to her. "You okay?" he asked.

Kristi looked at him, then shook her head. "Yeah, no, no, I'm not," she said, wiping the sniffles from her nose. "I miss him a lot, but I'm so angry at him. How could he leave me by myself to deal with all of this?"

Kristi's face contorted. More tears filled her eyes as she sobbed.

"You're not alone," Nash said, embracing her.

She buried her head in his chest and bawled. They stayed this way for a few moments before she gently nudged away from his chest. They locked eyes.

"You know," Kristi said, "you're a good cop, but a better man."

Nash smiled. "A lot of women been telling me that lately," he said.

Kristi giggled. "Let me guess, Francesca," she said.

Nash's smile grew until he chuckled. "What? You don't think I have other women in my life?"

Kristi poked her lips and cocked her head to the side.

"You feel better?" Nash asked her.

She nodded while drawing in a shaky breath. "Yeah, I do. For now at least," she said before playfully snatching the candy bar from Nash's hand.

"I knew you wanted that," Nash teased. "Chocolate is a comfort food for women."

"Shut up. I thought I chose the pretzels."

"Right."

They both laughed.

"Ready to get this all behind us?" Nash asked.

Kristi nodded. "I am," she said with a sigh.

"Well, let's do it," Nash said while guiding Kristi into the hallway.

EPILOGUE

Three months later, Nash found himself staring through the bars of a six-by-eight cell. He felt comfortable in his slacks, button-up shirt, and tie but couldn't believe how everything played out. He had a big break in his case. And it was all thanks to his favorite informant.

"Look, I told you everything," Tony said from within the jail cell. "Is it necessary to keep me here?"

"Calm down," Nash told him. "Had to make sure your information checked out."

Tony's eyes widened as he bounced his shoulders and gently shook his head. "Well, did it?"

"It did. We're picking the guy up now."

"Can I leave? I don't want 'em to see me here. He'll think I snitched on him."

Nash's eyebrows furrowed. "You did snitch on him."

"Yeah, but he don't know that."

Nash shook his head while unlocking the cell door. "C'mon, man."

He escorted Tony out of the holding cell area. Just as they entered the hall, a slimmer and seemingly taller Chris approached with a folder in hand.

"My officers got your guy," he said to Nash. "They're on their way to the station now." Chris gave Nash the folder, then nodded at Tony. "I can process his release, and get the other guy processed when he comes in. I know you have other things you need to do."

"Thank you, sergeant," Nash told him. "Think I'm gonna grab some lunch first, but he's all yours. You look good by the way. That yoga and dieting is working."

Chris smiled. "Oh, yeah?" he said, looking down at his midsection and patting his belly.

Tony sucked his teeth and shook his head.

"Ya'll have fun now," Nash said on his way down the hall.

"Yo, D," Chris called after him.

Nash turned around.

"We still on for the game next week, right?" Chris continued.

"The Hawks versus the Heat. Of course."

"Oh, I wanted to go to that game," Tony chimed in. "Can I go with ya'll?"

Both Nash and Chris laughed.

Nash continued down the hall toward a set of double doors. He used his keycard, then entered his passcode at the panel. The door buzzed, and he entered another hall before passing through another door and into the police station's main corridor. He landed in an office space with multiple cubicles. Stopping at the desk with his name on it, he opened the desk drawer and placed the folder Chris gave him inside. He left the cubicle, and just when he reentered the main corridor, he bumped into Moore. They both stood for a moment and forced a smile on their faces.

Nash nodded. "Detective Moore," he said.

"Detective Nash," Moore said.

They circled past each other. Moore entered the office area while Nash made his way to Barnhill's office. The door was cracked open. Nash poked his head inside. The lieutenant sat behind his desk with his phone to his ear. Nash waved, intending to duck back into the hall, but Barnhill beckoned him in with a wave of his own. The lieutenant concluded his call just before Nash made it to his desk.

"Detective Nash," he said. "What's going on?"

"Just wanted to let you know I got my guy," Nash said.

"The Richardson case?"

"Yep. Not only was his DNA all over the crime scene, his alibi doesn't check out. We have an eyewitness putting him at the scene during the time of the murder."

"Oh, is that why I saw Tony here earlier?"

"Yeah, but he's not the eyewitness. He knew someone who knew the eyewitness. After checking out their story, everything lines up."

Barnhill shrugged his lips. "Congratulations."

"Thanks. I'm on my way to lunch. I'll finish the paperwork and processing when I get back."

"Before you go," Barnhill said, standing from his desk. "Thank you."

Nash shrugged. "Imma detective now. Just doing my job."

"No." Barnhill circled around the desk. "I don't think I ever mentioned it, but you really saved the precinct working the Jackson case. Although you operated a little outside of protocol, it was still fine cop work."

"Thank you."

"The chief has been telling me for the last two months how thankful he is that we got in front of it."

"Was just tryna do the right thing."

Barnhill nodded as a smile arched on his face. "I know," he said. "Well, enjoy your lunch, my friend—oh, did you hear?"

"What?"

"Your friend, Ms. Bianchi, is getting released next month."

"Francesca? She's not my friend," Nash said before shrugging. "But I guess that's good for her. I'll see you when I get back."

He left the office and followed the corridor to the main entrance. He danced around a group of uniformed officers huddled near the door on his way outside. His eyes adjusted to the sun's glare and his body to the slight temperature increase. On his way to his car, he passed another uniformed officer and two civilians. A familiar silhouette approached from the opposite side of the passersby. Nash stopped, and so did the figure. He smiled when he realized who it was.

"Guess I should call you stranger now," he said.

"Guess I can call you the same," Kristi said.

She was wearing jeans and a long-sleeved shirt, similar clothes to what she wore the very first time they met.

"Haven't heard from you in about two months," Nash said.

"The phone works both ways, doesn't it?"

He stepped toward her. "You acted like you wanted some space," he said with a shrug.

Kristi stepped toward him. "So you just leave your friend alone?" she said.

Nash raised an eyebrow. "You consider us friends?"

She gently half-nodded and blinked her eyes once. A gesture that answered yes without fully admitting it.

The two were within arm's reach when Nash asked, "How have you been?"

Kristi sighed. "You know, some days are better than others," she said. "Spent some time with family, so that helped. Had time to come to terms with everything, and I feel better."

Nash nodded.

"What about you?" she continued. "How's everything in the life of Officer Nash?"

Nash smiled. "Well, it's actually Detective Nash now."

Kristi's eyes brightened. "Really? I beg your pardon, Detective Nash."

"Well, you know how I do."

The two laughed.

Kristi pursed her lips and stared at Nash. "I'm really proud of you. You deserve it," she said.

Nash stared back at her. "Thank you. Means a lot coming from you."

The two fixed on one another for a long moment.

"So what are you doing here?" Nash said, breaking their shared hypnotic gaze.

Kristi glanced at her feet. "Yeah, I came here to see someone," she said, pointing toward the station's entrance.

"Oh, Moore?"

"Yeah, well, no. Was actually hoping to run into you since I haven't seen you in a bit."

Nash smiled. Kristi smiled back.

"You hungry?" Nash asked.

"I could go for some grub."

"Okay, let's take my car. I know a place I think you'll like."

THANK YOU FOR READING

I have a favor to ask. If you have a moment, I would really appreciate it if you could leave a short review on the page where you purchased this book.

If you received this book through a promotion or gift, you can leave a review on Goodreads or Bookbub.

I'm thankful for you sharing your feedback about this book. It really helps new readers find this series.

Sign up for notifications of new books by Alex Cage and exclusive giveaways

www.AlexCage.com/signup

MORE BY ALEX CAGE

More books by Alex Cage. Have you read them all? Grab your next adventure today!

Orlando Black Series

Carolina Dance

Bayside Boom

Bet on Black

Leroy Silver Series

Contracts & Bullets

Aloha & Bullets

Politics Thieves & Bullets

Get the latest releases and exclusive giveaways, sign up to the Alex Cage Reader List.

www.AlexCage.com/signup

ABOUT THE AUTHOR

Alex Cage is a thriller author and passionate wordsmith who loves to blend his fascination with martial arts and travel with high-octane action and explosive adventures. He enjoys nothing more than entertaining his readers with death-defying missions, larger-than-life characters, and suspenseful stories that always find a way to keep you on your toes.

As the author of nearly a dozen titles, including the Orlando Black series and the Leroy Silver series, Alex combines his obsession for thrillers with a sprinkling of fantasy and sci-fi, so that readers will always find something to capture their imagination. He currently resides in North Carolina. When not writing his next novel, you can find him reading and practicing martial arts.

Find out more about Alex Cage (and get a free read):

www.alexcage.com
connect@alexcage.com

ALEX CAGE
CLEAN FAST-PACED ACTION THRILLERS

www.ingramcontent.com/pod-product-compliance
Lightning Source LLC
Chambersburg PA
CBHW030903200726
48289CB00003B/871